D1069170

The Redneck Bride

The Redneck Bride

a novel by

John Fergus Ryan

illustrations for this first edition by

John B. Ryan

August House/Little Rock
PUBLISHERS

Published 1982 by August House, Inc., Publishers,
1010 West Third Street, Little Rock, AR 72201
501-376-4516

First edition: October, 1982

ISBN: 0-935304-33-9 Hardback

Library of Congress Catalog Card Number: 82-70166
Ryan, John Fergus
The Redneck Bride: A Novel
Little Rock: August House
October, 1982

Part of this novel first appeared in *Penthouse* Magazine.

Dedicated to

Elizabeth Calvert

and

Laura Ingram

1

History and Geography of Bloat, Mississippi

Bloat, Mississippi lies thirty-one miles south of Memphis, Tennessee on State Improved Road Number 147 and is the second largest city in Titus County.

It was founded in 1874 by Colonel Washington T Bloat, then the richest man in north Mississippi, when he established a general store and hotel and built fifteen rent houses on the banks of tne Okipitta River, at the site of an old Indian trading camp.

Colonel Bloat made his fortune during the Civil War, selling cardboard shoes to the armies of both sides.

He was later a Mississippi State Senator.

The principal industries in Bloat, Mississippi are Titus County Wood Products, manufacturers of hickory axe handles; Carl McLathers Chemical Company, makers of Black Rascal House Paint; and Spatts "Big Boy" Foods, millers of Dixie Midget Corn Meal.

A prominent tourist attraction is the famous old Budley-Spuggs Home, late residence of Amanda Budley-Spuggs, music teacher and composer of a hymn, "When Sweet Jesus Climbs the Ladder, I'll be There," which was once sung on the radio.

Built in 1946, the house was one of the first in Titus County to have interiors of Gypsum wall board. The Budley-Spuggs Home is maintained by the City of Bloat and the floorboards are guaranteed sound. Open Monday afternoons. Admission five cents.

Bloat High School's colors are blue and white and are immortalized in the famous football cheer:

Blue and White,
Fight, Fight!

Blue and White,
Fight, Fight!

Yeah, Yeah,
Who are we?

Bloat, Mississippi,
Can't you see?

The population of Bloat, Mississippi is 4,325.

2

Rixie Leaptrot and Bunny Whitesides Hit Town

LAKE CATCH-A-CAT. THREE MILES. ADMISSION ONE DOLLAR. BLOAT, MISSISSIPPI. HOME OF YVONNE HANGMAN. FIVE MILES. PANGBURN'S BOAT DOCK. MINNOWS. BEER.

Signs along the road were bright flashes in the summer morning as a late model pickup truck, painted Sea Foam Tan and Versailles Green, with MATHENY BUTANE lettered on the doors of the cab, sped north to Bloat.

The driver, fifty, fat, in steel-toe safety shoes, Western straw hat, cotton khaki wash pants and a white Arrow dress shirt with heavy starch, was red of face, hypertensive and bespectacled.

He had a bullhorn in his hand, powered off the cigarette lighter on the dashboard, and whenever he came to landmarks along the road, he slowed down and called out something about them through the bullhorn, to two men who were riding in the bed of the pickup, in among some old junk tires, a burned-out power lawn mower, a fifty-pound sack of yellow onions and two five-gallon drums of PLYDROX, a good pre-emergent herbicide. The two men were pinned in place in the truck bed by the gaze of an evil-tempered Redbone hound who had a painful gum disease.

"Old Landis place!" yelled the driver through the bullhorn, as they passed a farmhouse. "Cane Creek...mule farm...Simmons... peaches ... Holdup ... catch 'em."

Information like that, all along the way.

"Chinaberry tree ... Baptist Church."

The two men in the truck bed could not understand what the driver was saying. His words were carried away on the wind, for he was going seventy miles an hour in a sixty-mile zone.

Two miles outside of Bloat, the driver slowed down to a stop and turned left off the road into the gates of the New Carmel Hope Cemetery.

"I want you all to see this," he said, through the bullhorn. "The new cemetery. Gilliad got full up, had to open this one. New, ten years ago. Just ten years and already over three hundred Christians sleeping here. I won't stop, I'll just drive on through."

New Carmel Hope Cemetery was seven and a half acres in size with a narrow, twisting, rutted dirt road coursing through it. There were over three hundred marble headstones, all of the same design, the same size and thickness, about two feet high, three feet long and tapering into the same width at the top.

A colorful arrangement of plastic flowers, running three feet in length, decorated the top of each tombstone and was held in place by wire teeth.

"See them flowers on top of each grave rock?" asked the driver. "Look at them! Have you never seen nothing prettier?"

He drove on slowly until he came to the principal artistic attraction of the cemetery, a poured-concrete statue of an heroic shepherd surrounded by poured-concrete lambs, also heroic.

"The Shepherd and the Lambikins," said the driver. "Made in Dallas, Texas. Donated by the Wheat brothers. They made their money in wholesale beer and cigarettes. They put up that statue to try and make it up to the Lord."

There was no more time to waste and the driver headed back to the road. At the gates, he stopped, opened the cab door, stood on the running board and looked back at the cemetery. He picked up the bullhorn and shouted "REST IN PEACE! GOD LOVE YOU!" He then saluted, got back behind the wheel and shot away toward town.

Three or four more times along the way he identified the sights. He was going so fast that just part of what he said was audible to the men in the truck bed.

"... farm ... Pola bear ... Fire ... tree ... fifteen killed."

One of the passengers, the elder of the two, put his mouth up to the ear of the other and shouted:

"I'm sure surprised we got out of that cemetery alive. I thought he was fixin' to kill us both! He's got the look of a crazy!"

The other man nodded in agreement.

"One of these days," said the older man, "I'm gonna be well enough off I don't have to hitch a ride with just any damn crazy suh mitch that comes along."

A sign on the roadside read: ENTERING THE CITY OF BLOAT. HOME OF YVONNE HANGMAN. A large billboard, set back a few yards off the road, five big spotlights overhanging it, read: BLOAT, MISSISSIPPI. WELCOME. FOUR STAR CITY. PROSPERITY! FRIENDLINESS! INDUSTRY! AGRICULTURE! Bloat Booster Club. Meets Spit Cafe. Friday.

The driver passed the hickory-axe-handle factory and the consolidated school before stopping at Korky's Kone 'n' Kola, at the south end of town. Next door was the Dot Oil Company, an automobile service station in a low concrete-block building, its driveways caked with old, wasted oil. Across the street was the water tower and storage tank, two hundred feet tall, with "CLAS [sic] of 1967" spraypainted across it.

The driver got out of the truck. His knees were stiff and he had trouble walking. He smiled at the two men in the back of the truck.

"If you two's still lookin for a plate lunch, then that's your spot, right chonder. The Spit Cafe," he said.

The two men stood up, brushed the road dust off their clothing, then jumped off the truck. Their quick movements upset the hound. He lunged for them, but missed.

It was his age. Time was, he could have grabbed them both, and then some. When he was young, he had run with the pack at Parchman Farm, the Mississippi State Prison.

"Mister, your dog like to have went for me," said the older passenger.

"Ole Crawdad? He's skittish, right enough."

"I'm Rixie Leaptrot," said the older man, extending his hand.

"Pinky Winkler," said the driver.

Rixie Leaptrot was thin and wiry, not quite five feet tall, his face lined, wrinkled, and browned by the sun. He had thin hair, a jutting chin and an aura of wiliness about him.

"We're much obliged to you for picking us up back there in Arkansas," said Rixie Leaptrot. "Don't know what them State Police told you ..."

"A man's past ain't none of my bidness," said Pinky Winkler. "It's the Lord he'll have to answer to."

"We was run out of Arkansas ..."

"It ain't none of my bidness! You'll have to settle up with the

Lord!"

Pinky Winkler reached into his shirt pocket and pulled out a tract.

"WHY NOT SPEND ETERNITY ON EASY STREET INSTEAD OF BOURBON STREET?" was its title.

He slipped it into Rixie Leaptrot's hand with a behind-his-back motion, like it was dirty, like he was up to something, then touched his hat brim and got back into the truck.

"This is as far as I go," he said. "If it's a plate lunch you want, you can't beat the Spit."

"What's the name of this town?" asked Rixie Leaptrot.

"Bloat, Miss'sippi. Up and coming!"

Pinky Winkler gunned the truck's engine and shot gravel. Rixie Leaptrot watched the truck disappear.

"That bogus suh mitch!" he said. "If he was such a Christian, why didn't he let us ride in the cab?"

Rixie Leaptrot took a handkerchief out of his pocket and wiped his forehead. He was wearing a long-sleeved, apricot-colored, puckered rayon shirt, heavy wool winter pants and cowboy boots with the soles nearly worn through.

"You hear what that man said, Bunny?" he asked the younger man. "We're in Bloat, Mississippi!"

Bunny Whitesides was young, twenty-five at the most, handsome, lean, muscular, with long blonde hair and big white teeth. He wore blue jeans, old, faded, torn, skin-tight, and a white cotton T-shirt.

Rixie Leaptrot and Bunny looked down the length of Main Street, which was also State Improved Road Number 147. It was nearly noon, on a hot Friday in late August. A few people moved, here and there, along the dusty street.

"If this ain't the most unlovely town in all northwest Mississippi, then I'm the Pagan Love Song," said Rixie Leaptrot. "A whole town smelling of kerosene! A whole town with bad roofs!"

Bunny smiled. He picked up a Ford automobile by the back bumper and held its rear end up a foot off the ground.

"We ain't got time for your skylarking!" said Rixie Leaptrot. "Set that car down and let's get us that plate lunch."

They had to walk the length of Main Street to get to the Spit Cafe — past Slipweasel and Drat Mercantile Company; Twyla's Flower Dell (its window filled with three-foot-long arrangements of plastic flowers, with wire teeth for clipping them to "grave rocks"); Cliff Chickle's Body Shop; Al's Meat Market (Hogs, Cattle Killed, Chilled, Cut, Wrapped); Honeycutt Crop Loans: Faoud Honeycutt, Sec. Treas.; Swan Bagley, Atty. and Notary Public; the office of the *Titus County Tomcat*; a vacant lot with a sign which said "I BUY

COTTON GINS. Col. G. S. Roosevelt. Marked Tree, Arkansas"; the Tenant Farmers Bank and Trust Company; and RAFE MUNGER, LAND DEALS.

Then, the Spit Cafe!

The Spit Cafe had a plaster pig, revolving over a bed of red lights made to look like glowing coals, on a fake spit in one of the two front windows.

Hence the name.

There was a four-color illustration painted on the other window which showed a little fat man with a big nose, wearing a derby hat, peering out from behind a hamburger that was as big as he was.

Underneath the illustration was the slogan: WORLD'S LARGEST HAMBURGER. TAKES AN HOUR TO EAT.

Rixie Leaptrot and Bunny went inside. The essence of a good fly spray hit them. They sat down at the counter and looked around. There were fifty loaves of bread stacked on the floor in the corner by the cash register. Framed photographs of the owner's three children hung on the wall, next to the cans of chili that had been stacked in a pyramid. Seven or eight mounted fish, mostly rough stuff, scrud or brakes taken from the Okipitta River, hung along the walls.

It was cool, quiet. Early. The lunch hour rush had not yet begun. There were a few loungers, drinking beer.

Coco Seifert, daughter of a rich planter in the Delta, now in her late fifties, thrice divorced, wearing a gold lamé jumpsuit and gold lamé shoes that curled at the toe, was sitting at a table, staring off, recalling her youth, long ago, her debut, parties, Sophie Newcomb, old money, Memphis society, the Greenville Cotillion, New Orleans, and The Sugar Exchange.

Buster, the routeman for Fay's Nuts and Chips, out of Jackson, was restocking the wire racks and flirting with her.

"I sure would like to get next to you, Miss Coco!" he said.

"You're too old for me, young man," she said.

She went back to her reverie: her girlhood — two cousins and the raft they sailed on Lake Ferguson, a raft they named The Happy Water Lilly.

A young couple — he dressed in a dark suit, white shirt, floral-print necktie, black shoes from Italy, lots of glittering jewelry, cuff links, tie clasp, key chains, frat pins; she in lime-colored stretch pants and a yellow sleeveless blouse — sat at a table in the back, next to the MEN'S.

Her hair was long, worn in a pony tail and dyed a gloomy black. Her skin was Chalk and her eyebrows were heightened — black,

The hamburger took an hour to eat.

black, black.

There was a space between her two front teeth big enough to stick a pencil through.

Rixie Leaptrot and Bunny squirmed on their seats at the counter. All of the fixtures in the Spit Cafe — the tables, chairs, the floor, the counter top and four feet up along the walls — were made of oak, under many coats of cloudy varnish. Everything was sticky.

"Stickiest place I've ever been in," said Rixie Leaptrot. "You can't set your elbow down without it pulls when you try to move it."

The waitress appeared and wiped the counter in front of the two men with a greasy cloth. She was sixty-three, had red hair, bad teeth and too many rolls of fat around her neck. One look at her and you knew waiting table at the Spit was the best job she had ever had.

"Menus?" she asked.

"I don't need a menu," said Rixie Leaptrot. "Honey, I'm red-eyed and nervous and I got the hungry shakes. I'm mean with them! I been dreaming of right now for three months! I got it all down in my head! I want some good eats! I ain't had nothing but grits and fried bologna since before Decoration Day!"

"Sounds to me like you been in the pen," said the waitress. "That's what they feeds in the pen. Least, that's what all my husband's people say. That's they way they tells it."

Rixie Leaptrot beckoned the waitress close.

"The pen's right!" he said. "That's just where we was. Over in Arkansas, just crost the river. Three months on the county road force. We served our time and got turned loose with ten dollars apiece, but before we could eat it up, the State Police over there, they run us out of Arkansas! Put us on the back of a pickup crossing into Mississippi before we could get so much as a Whiz bar. So here we are, with ten dollars apiece and we aim to eat it all up and worry about later later."

"What was you in the pen for?" asked the waitress. "Boot laig?"

"Nem'mine," said Rixie Leaptrot.

"I was just asking. What'll it be?"

"Bring me your regular catfish dinner and a plate of chili beans, a fried peach pie, a glass of sugared tea, a pint of sweet milk, some fresh picked greens, buckwheats and baby links, a bowl of split pea, new potatoes, thickenin' gravy, a whole cole drink, a cheeseburger with pickle, mustard and onion, a BLT on toast, butterbeans and bacon, a deep-fried minute steak, a speckled trout, a jar of honey, steam cabbage, liver and onions, banana pudding, fried ham, apricots and hot Irish stew, fried eggs, chicken legs, milk shakes, hot cakes, cracklin' bread, tomato salad, sweet potato pie, hot biscuits, some clean penny candy, an order of fries and a Swiss on rye, and for dessert, bring me six or eight Dixie cups, them kind with a movie star's picture on the inside of the top ..."

"That'd be some good eatin', all right," said the waitress.

"Bring it! Everything!" said Rixie Leaptrot.

"You serious?"

"I'm serious!"

"Well, that's too bad, 'cause we don't handle the fourth part of all that. All we got is a little ole plate lunch, a meat and three veg'tables."

"That's what I was afraid of!" sputtered Rixie Leaptrot in a fury.

"I might find you some hot biscuits."

"That's what I was afraid of," repeated Rixie Leaptrot.

"We got the Shopper's Special. Mock mock turtle soup and black-eye pea pancakes."

Rixie Leaptrot waved his hand to dismiss the Shopper's Special and accidentally knocked over a pint fruit jar containing an arrangement of Dwarf Mingles and Belle Verandah.

"You don't have to get mad," said the waitress. "This ain't the Service Cafe in Memphis!"

"I ain't mad. Bring me the plate lunch. Nothing ever works out!"

"What does he want?" asked the waitress.

"Bunny? Bring him the same."

Bunny grabbed Rixie Leaptrot's sleeve, looked him in the eyes and made a few swift passes in the air with his fingers.

"The Kid says he wants sorghum on his biscuits."

"Can't he talk?" asked the waitress.

"Bunny talk? No sir, not a word! He's what they call a mute. Can't talk but he can hear like a bell."

"Well, ain't that the awflest thing. I'M AWFUL SORRY, BUNNY!"

Bunny nodded. The waitress left to place their order in the kitchen. Music — "Dirty Mushtash" — was coming from the jukebox:

I got corn mush in my mushtash,
and the dang thing's drawing flies.

I can't breathe through my noseholes,
and the flies lite in my eyes.

Gotta wash my mushtash
Gotta wash my mushtash

Or the County will condemn it,
and me, too!

My face is clean,
My hands are washed,
My ears are scrubba dubbed.

It's just that when
I cleaned me up
My mushtash dub was flubbed.

Gotta wash my mushtash
Gotta wash my mushtash

Gotta comb and brush and scrape it through,

Or the County will condemn it,
and me, too!

Bunny went over to the jukebox and picked it up over his head with one arm. He held it above his head, smiling.

"Bunny!" said Rixie Leaptrot. "Here, now! Put down that joot box! Come back over here and sit down!"

Bunny did as he was told. He set the jukebox down gently and it resumed playing "Dirty Mushtash."

Buster, the routeman for Fay's Nuts and Chips, inserted a quarter in the juke box. "Now we gonna hear some real music!" he said, and punched "Meat Momma."

The lyrics of "Meat Momma" consisted of the words "Meat Momma" repeated fifty-three times, followed by a Calypso bridge, then back to First for another fifty-three times.

Bunny was resting his head in his hand, his elbow on the counter.

"That boy looks sleepy," said the waitress. "ARE YOU SLEEPY, SUGAH?" she asked.

Bunny nodded.

"That is the sleepin'est boy," said Rixie Leaptrot. "We drove over here in the back of a pickup truck. Just made for sight-seeing! But that Bunny! He slept right through the Okipitta River!"

"Yvonne Hangman was that way," said the waitress. "When she was a little girl, she'd go to sleep right here in the Spit, right slap in the middle of the supper rush."

"Who is Yvonne Hangman?" asked Rixie Leaptrot. "Since I hit town, I ain't seen nothing but 'HOME OF YVONNE HANGMAN.'"

"You don't know who Yvonne Hangman is?" asked the waitress. "Where you been all your life? Yvonne Hangman is a movie star, that's who she is!"

"Movie star?" repeated Rixie Leaptrot.

"She's the only little girl from Bloat ever to make it big in movies."

"Never heard of her."

"Never heard of her? Didn't you never hear of *Moonshiner's Daughter*?"

"Nope."

"Well, that was her big one. Came out about five years ago. They showed it at ever drive-in in the country."

The waitress served the plate lunches: fillet of sea trout, pickled beets, baby limas, shredded lettuce with French dressing, and a saucer of coconut custard.

"I don't like pickle beets," said Rixie Leaptrot.

"I can give you cream corn or mash potatoes," said the waitress.

Rixie Leaptrot and Bunny Whitesides were just getting into their shredded lettuce salads when the couple sitting at the back, near the MEN'S, started getting loud.

"Quit foon with mah tiddies!" said the girl with the space between her teeth. "They's tender!"

"They's tender?" asked the young man she was with, he in the dark suit and all the jewelry. "Who's been foon with 'em?"

The girl stood up, brushed Beer Nuts off her lap, and stormed out. He followed.

The waitress leaned over the counter to Rixie Leaptrot and confided, "There goes a crying shame. That boy was Rafe Munger, Jr. His daddy's Rafe Munger, Land Deals."

"I seen his sign," said Rixie Leaptrot. "I bet he's as crooked as the hairs in a gypsy's nose."

"He is that! Rafe Munger owns ever rent house in town and he'll read you out if you get as much as a month behind in your rent. He did that to us, me and my husband, had us read out right slap in the middle of last winter and my husband is disable to work. I mean to tell!"

Rixie Leaptrot shook his head in disbelief.

"That Rafe, Jr., he's spawled!" said the waitress. "Them rich kids is all spawled! That's what they are! Spawled rotten!"

"There ain't no such of a thing as a happy rich kid," agreed Rixie Leaptrot.

"What makes me so all fired mad," said the waitress, "is Rafe, Jr. is fixing to get married and that girl with him is not the one he's gonna marry!"

"Not his bride-to-be?"

"I'll say not! That was just little ole Sula Measles from out at Four Points. He's fixing to marry Davy Sue Merkle a week from tomorrow at two o'clock in the afternoon. I'm sure glad she didn't walk in here while they were sitting back by the MEN'S. I wouldn't want her to get hurt for anything in the world! She's just about the nicest girl there is! And smart! Made nothing but A all the way through high! And you don't make an A in Shorthand from Miss Effie Chad Reed unless you knows it!

"Davy Sue's gonna be fixed for life, marrying Rafe, Jr. You talk about money! They say Rafe Munger is worth nearly a hundred thousand dollars! And her mother waited table right here in the Spit until her verrycose veins got too bad ..."

Music came from the juke box:

Quit snarlin', darlin' ...
Let's stop this silly quarrellin' ...

The waitress kept on talking. "...and Rafe, Jr., here in the Spit, right out in the open, loving up another ..."

"He's no-count looking," said Rixie Leaptrot. "I never have had any use for a man with a harelip."

"Well, you can hardly see it through his mushtash," said the waitress.

"Dresses well, though," admitted Rixie Leaptrot.

"That's the old man's doing. Rafe Munger. It's him with the taste in clothes. He makes Rafe, Jr. dress up to it. Why, Rafe, Jr. would go as long as two weeks without a haircut if the old man didn't stay after him.

"MORE COFFEE, BUNNY? What's his name? It ain't 'Bunny,' for real, is it?"

"It is, for real," said Rixie Leaptrot. "Bunny Alphonso Whitesides. Me, I'm Rixie Leaptrot. My folks was circus people."

The waitress cast her eyes toward the Heavens and held her arms out straight at her sides.

"I'm Mom," she said, smiling crazily. "Everybody calls me 'Mom,' God love 'em!"

More music from the juke box:

... soggy pretzels and lukewarm beer.
Why, oh why, am I sitting here ... ?

''Everybody calls me 'Mom,' God love 'em!''

"Are you planning to stay in Bloat?" asked Mom.
"Prolly not," said Rixie Leaptrot. "Prolly not."
"Have some more coffee?"
"Just a mite."

3

Duane Yancey Plans To Take Bloat By Storm

At the same time Rixie Leaptrot was in the Spit talking to Mom, Duane Yancey was heading south on the highway from Memphis to Bloat to apply for a job as reporter for the *Titus County Tomat*.

WELCOME TO MISSISSIPPI — THE MAGNOLIA STATE.
ARKABUTLA CUTOFF — NEXT EXIT.

South, south, south.

ENID LAKE JAYCEES MEET AT PARKER'S TWAT HOUSE CAFE. EVERY SECOND TUESDAY.

Nothing gets the attention of a Memphis State University graduate faster than ENID LAKE JAYCEES.

Duane Yancey had great self-confidence. He was twenty-three years old with a degree in Communications. He would get the job at the *Titus County Tomat*, make a success of it, join the Bloat Jaycees and work hard for them.

Eleven-thirty in the morning and his new car was performing

beautifully. The floorboard seemed too hot but the man at the dealership had told him it was supposed to get hot. That was the way it was designed. But still, surely not so hot it burned your shoes!

He was glad he had bought a new car before getting fired at Yak Brothers Auto Seat Covers, but he wished he had had the foresight to get a set of those waffle-surface, clear plastic Starliner seat covers while he still had his employee discount.

Yancey had written copy for Yak Brothers' seat cover catalogues until he had been fired there. This was the second job he had lost since his graduation thirteen months ago. If they had given him a little longer to learn, he could have caught on and done a real ball-of-fire job.

Before that, there had been the job at the First Plastic Ozan Corporation, researching customer acceptance of their products — plastic dish drainers and pet feeding and drinking dishes.

Fired there, too.

Duane Yancey was one of those people who always has money, even when unemployed. His car note was paid ahead, he lived at home and owed no rent, and he was not yet up to his limit with VISA or Master Charge.

Yancey also had a lot of new, flashy, double-knit clothes. This morning, for instance, for his interview at one-thirty in the afternoon, he wore a yellow short-sleeved shirt, a bright red necktie with a pattern, maroon slacks, a double-breasted blue blazer with brass buttons, and red, white and blue wingtip shoes.

Yancey had heard about the opening at the *Titus County Tomcat* through the journalism department at Memphis State University. He had telephoned the publisher, Elmo "Tubby" Turmath and arranged an interview with him.

He hit Bloat about noon, found the *Tomcat* office without any trouble, drove around town to get the feel of the place and then had lunch at the Spit Cafe: fiillet of sea trout, turnip greens, mashed potatoes, cornbread, coconut pudding and two cartons of chocolate milk. As he paid the check, he was aware of the curious and unfriendly stares he was getting from the others in the Spit. He nodded in the direction of a table full of Bloat businessmen and said,

"Hoddy."

They nodded back and Yancey left the Spit. *No matter*, he thought. *If I get the job, I'll get in with them.*

He arrived at the *Tomcat* office ten minutes before his appointment, parked in the visitors' lot and took his scrapbook of by-lined newspaper clippings, from his high school and college days, out of the back seat.

As he was approaching the building, a big, meaty man of about forty-five came out of the *Tomcat* office, carrying a bag of golf clubs. He saw Yancey.

"Can I he'p you?" he asked, setting down the golf clubs.

"My name's Yancey. I'm looking for Mr. Turmath."

"What foah?"

"I've got an appointment to see him about a job."

"I'll be a suh mitch!" said the big man. "I clean forgot about it. Lucky you was to catch me. Come on in! Goff can wait. Some things can't wait. Now if it was something to do with pussy, that couldn't wait, but goff can wait!"

He laughed insanely.

Turmath was dumb-looking — like a big sheep. His eyes were almost swollen shut with facial fat. He wore a cotton pullover shirt with a little alligator over the breast pocket, powder-blue slacks and white leather shoes. His thinning blonde hair was cut close and he used a good oil on it. A curious scent emanated from him that seemed to be a mixture of a common aftershave and cigar smoke.

"Come on into my office," he said to Yancey, after they had already walked into his office. "What's you take in your coffee?"

He had a coffeepot on an electric hot plate. "Me, I like mine like I like my wimmin, hot and black," he said.

Again, he laughed insanely.

The office was panelled in speckled pecan and the walls were hung with trophies of Turmath's football career and framed certificates from luncheon service clubs in town.

"Aw right, now. Set down there and sell me," said Turmath.

Yancey produced his scrapbook of clippings and gave Turmath a written resumé of his education and past job experience. Turmath turned the pages of the scrapbook hurriedly, not taking the trouble to actually read any of it.

"Looks like you lost evah job you evah held, boy," said Turmath, after he glanced at the resumé. "How was it you come to get let out at that last one, the seat-cover place?"

"I had a personality conflict, I guess. With some of the salesmen."

"America's built on sales," said Turmath. "Sales's what made America great."

He glanced back at the scrapbook. "You say you got your college?" asked Turmath. "I played college ball." He turned and swept his arm over the room of trophies, then went back to looking at the clippings.

"Where was it you went?" he asked.

"Memphis State," said Yancey.

"Mif'fis State!" spat Turmath. "I went to Oklahoma A & M. I was there in the big years! Back when it meant something! How

Tubby Turmath smelled of a common aftershave.

about you? Did you play ball? You don't look big enough to make a football player."

"I didn't have time to play ball. I went in more for frat life."

"Which one you belong to?"

"Sigma Chi."

"Good ole Sigma Chi. I was a Delta Kappa. I always said, I don't think a man can call his college life complete unless he was a member of a social fraternity."

He continued looking over the samples of Yancey's work. At last he closed the scrapbook.

"You ain't exactly what I'm looking for," said Turmath.

"Don't say that, Mr. Turmath! Inside, I'm the hardest driving never-quitter you ever saw!"

"I'm looking for a man with more experience on a weekly paper."

"I wish you'd give me a chance to prove myself, Mr. Turmath."

"But you got one thing going for you that I like. You got weak eyes. If there's one thing I like for my help to have, it's weak eyes!"

"Weak eyes?"

"When can you start?"

"Today! Right away!"

"You got a place to stay?"

"Not yet."

"You can get a room at Mrs. Tate's. Mrs. Tait Tate. Somebody around town'll show you where she lives."

"Thanks, Mr. Turmath!"

Tubby Turmath stepped over the door of his office. "Frank!" he yelled. "Frank, get your butt in here, boy!"

A thin, frazzled young man appeared.

"Yes, sir, Mr. Tubby!"

"This here is Frank, the City Editor," said Turmath to Yancey.

The two young men shook hands.

"I just hired this boy to work for the *Tomcat*," said Turmath to Frank. "Show him around, take him over to the funeral home, get him settled, then put his ass to work."

"Yes, sir, Mr. Tubby!" said Frank.

"If anybody comes looking for me, I'll be playing goff."

"Yes, sir, Mr. Tubby!" said Frank.

Frank took Yancey into the front office of the *Tomcat* and showed him a desk.

"That'll be yours," he said. "You can use that typewriter over yonder."

"OK," said Yancey.

"You from Mif'fis?" asked Frank.

"Right!"

"I hear you can get mix drinks up there."
"About three, four years now."
"Mif'fis must be somethin' else!"
"You the City Editor?"
"That, and I drive the hearse when they's a funeral."
"Funeral?"
"Mutt Brothers Funeral Home, right across the parking lot. It's owned by the *Tomcat*. Mr. Tubby runs them both."
"I didn't plan on getting mixed up with a funeral home."
"I drive the hearse and sometimes help out the embalmer, but I'm inside a writer. I been sending off stuff to *True Detective.* Not good enough yet, I guess. But you wait! You wait until they's a big axe murder around here someplace, and see if I don't get it wrote up in *True Detective!*"
"You ought to move up to Memphis, if you want to write. Try the papers up there."
"I'd like to, but I can't. My wife, she don't want to leave her people. Her name's Juney Garland, like the star."
"You mean JUDY Garland? Her name was JUDY."
"I know that! But her people didn't! They thought it was JUNEY! They was that dumb!"
"Oh."
"Come on over and I'll show you the funeral home."
The two men walked across the parking lot.
"This here is the Mutt Brothers Motor Vista," said Frank, indicating the asphalt paved parking lot where they were standing. "Over yonder, where those benches and them Jesus statues are, that's the Sculpture Garden."
They entered the funeral parlor.
"You want a Co-Cola?" asked Frank.
"I guess so."
Frank put a coin in the vending machine and there was heard the sound of gears meshing and works churning; then a frosty cold jumbo bottle of Sun Gold Grape Soda appeared.
He was perplexed.
"I punched a Coke!" he said.
A high school couple, a boy of sixteen and a girl no older, wearing MASTER and SLAVE cotton shirts, souvenirs of Panama City, Florida, entered and greeted Frank.
"We'd like to see Gran'daddy Wellborn," said the boy.
Frank led them to the right room, then returned to Duane Yancey. The two young men stood there, together, a moment.
"You married?" asked Frank.
"No."
"How old are you?"

"Twenty-three."

"Twenty-three and not married. You're sure one lucky suh mitch!" Frank raised the bottle of Sun Gold Grape Soda in salute. "Here's hoping your luck runs," he said.

"You don't have it so bad, except for him," said Yancey, nodding toward Tubby Turmath's office.

"Mr. Tubby? He'll treat you right. He married into all this. He was just another pore boy like me before he married Mona Mutt."

"Marry money. That's how you do it."

"That's what my sister Davy Sue is fixing to do. She's getting married to Rafe Junior Munger. Saturday, a week."

"Who's Rafe Junior Munger?"

"He's a no-count suh mitch, from way back, but his ole man's got money and gonna have more!"

"Maybe some of it'll rub off on you."

"That's what I'm figgerin'. If it don't, I may move on up to Mif'fis. A fella was around here the other day, telling me I could get on at National Burial Insurance, working a debit."

"Say, before I forget, can you tell me where a Mrs. Tate lives? Turmath said I could rent a room from her."

"Sure. Come on. I'll show you."

Rafe, Jr. had been drunk for one year.

4

Sula Measles and Rafe, Jr. Go on an Outing

Sula Measles left the Spit Cafe, with Rafe, Jr. following her. Just outside the door, she bumped into an old man in bib overalls, who was delivering a crate of live chickens to the Chinaman's store, next to the Spit. The old man looked at Sula Measles as she passed him, and said aloud, to no one in particular:

"There go the biggest tits on a white woman in Bloat, Mississippi!"

Sula opened the door of her new car, a sporty little Pimp, which was parked at the curb, and sat down in the driver's seat. She had just bought the car from Boxer's Imports in Memphis and got forty-eight months at a hundred and eighty-three dollars and forty-seven cents a month. Sula did factory work in Memphis, making dog food at a cereal mill and her take-home pay was over two hundred dollars a week. She had been there eight months and was up for promotion to inspector.

A delivery truck from the Nat Buring Packing Company in Memphis pulled up in front of the Chinaman's store at just that moment and blocked Sula against the curb.

The truck driver started unloading salt bellies.

Sula wanted to make a quick getaway from Rafe, Jr., but she would not have been able to even if the delivery truck had not pinned her in, for her bosom had got snagged in the steering wheel of the sports car and she had to suck in her breath and struggle a moment to free herself.

She was built like a little pouter pigeon, with breasts that snagged in the steering wheel. She could not push the driver's seat back any more. It was already as far back as it would go. The front seat was touching the back seat now.

Rafe, Jr., in his navy blue suit and white starched shirt, hair slicked down, his harelip white with rage, ran up in front of the Pimp, planted his hand on the hood, pivoted on it and opened the door opposite the driver's seat and got in.

"What are you doing in here with me?" asked Sula Measles, angrily. "You ain't going nowhere with me! If you want to marry that little adding machine of a Davy Sue Merkle, you ain't going to ride in my car!"

Rafe, Jr. had had too much premium beer and not enough food. He had been drunk every day since he graduated from Ole Miss a year ago.

"Don't chide me, Sula Jean!" he said. "That marrying Davy Sue, that's something she and my daddy cooked up. He wants me to marry her because she can add up a column of figures in her head quicker than a man with a machine."

"Get out of this car! I mean it, you peckerwood!"

Sula Jean and Rafe, Jr. had been going together off and on before Davy Sue Merkle had entered the picture. They had even been off on trips together. She would drive over to Oxford, Mississippi, when Rafe, Jr. had been in school there, and they would go off together someplace for the weekend. Once, they had even gone to the Dog Track in West Memphis, Arkansas, and Sula Jean had won fifty dollars on a Quinella.

"Come on, Sula Jean," begged Rafe, Jr. "Let's drive out to the Barrow Pits. For one last time!"

"You had your last time, Mr. Rafe Munger, Jr.! From now on, you can spin your time with Miss Davy Sue Merkle! You can go the Barrow Pits with her and spin the whole night looking for *her* tiddies!"

Como Wing, the Chinaman's son, had come out of the store and was watching the truck driver as he unloaded the salt bellies. He had a broom in his hand.

Salt bellies are slabs of white pork fat with thin streaks of lean. They are about two inches thick and two feet wide and four or five feet long. Sometimes they still have the teats on them.

Salt belly is a staple of the diet in Bloat, Mississippi.

The truck driver finished stacking the bellies on the sidewalk, a sheet of brown paper between each one, and handed Como Wing an invoice which read, "Ten salt bellies @ 24½ cents a pound. Six hundred ten pounds and eight ounces." He wanted Como Wing to sign for receipt of that much salt belly.

"Wait a minute," said Como Wing, and he began sweeping the salt bellies with his broom. He swept one side of a belly until he had swept off all the loose salt, then he had the truck driver turn the belly over and he swept off the other side. He swept all ten bellies, both sides, and brushed off a lot of salt. Then he had the driver re-weigh the bellies on the scale in front of the store.

The total, now less the salt, was nearly six pounds lighter.

When the truck driver adjusted the invoice to show the new net weight, Como Wing signed the invoice.

Sula Jean and Rafe, Jr. were still arguing, and the men in front of the Chinaman's store, the matter of the salt bellies out of the way, turned to watch them. The old man with the crate of chickens, who was a Mr. Ledbetter, now had an audience and repeated, "There sits the biggest tits on a white woman in Bloat, Mississippi!"

That Mr. Ledbetter! He *would* drive a joke in the ground.

"Let's get out of here!" said Sula Jean. "That old man's saying something nasty about me!"

The delivery truck was gone and she started the engine and slowly pulled away from the curb and headed south on Main Street.

"Stop at the bootlegger's," said Rafe, Jr., and Sula Jean pulled over, in front of a state-licensed package liquor store. It was not really a bootlegger's. The state had had legal liquor for several years, but people in Mississippi still call the place they buy their liquor "the bootlegger's" out of respect for tradition.

Rafe, Jr. went inside and bought a fifth of Wild Turkey bourbon and a six-pack of Seven-Up. He swayed as he paid the clerk.

"You ought to slow down, Rafe, Jr.," said the clerk, an old man named Roon Bodcaw, who had worked as a switchman for the Illinois Central Railroad in Chicago until he retired. "You ought to slow down. A young fella like you."

"Shut up, you old fool!" said Rafe, Jr., and he staggered back outside, leaving his change on the counter.

Something had happened to Sula Jean while she was waiting, something had softened her heart, and she agreed to go out to the Barrow Pits with Rafe, Jr. for one more time, the last one before he got married. She drove down Main Street, past the water tower, turned right at the Firecracker Stand — WORLD'S LARGEST FIREWORKS! CHERRY BOMBS AS BIG AS LABRADOR RETRIEVERS! — and headed down a dirt road, out in the county to the Barrow Pits.

The Barrow Pits were where the young people of Bloat, Mississippi went to "court." They were deep holes in the ground surrounded by tall mounds of dirt, holes made years ago by some company that dug them out to get at gravel or shale. In the years since, the pits had filled up with seep water from the creeks around them and were now deep pools of greenish-yellow stagnant water, filled with all kinds of rough fish — gar, scrud, brakes and grunions.

Grunions are little snakes with dog-like paws and are caught all along the rivers in Mississippi and can even be caught in salt water around Gulfport and Biloxi. They are some kind of prehistoric throwback, and that is what you do with one if you catch it, you throw it back. Grunions are that ugly and not good for eating or anything.

It was a short drive from the Firecracker Stand to the Barrow Pits. Sula Jean turned this way and that on the narrow roads among the mounds of dirt until she came to her favorite courting spot, a little recess where she could park and not be seen, but still see the road and not get caught by the sheriff's men, who patrolled the Barrow Pits, now and then, to run off courters, not that they were not out there themselves on their days off.

The Pimp was too small for Sula Jean and Rafe, Jr. to do anything inside it. They got out and climbed up a hill and Rafe, Jr. poured himself a drink, Wild Turkey and Seven-Up, in a white plastic cup. Sula Jean was not drinking.

"I quit drinking whiskey when I got Saved," she said. "I'll drink beer but I won't drink whiskey, because it's the hard stuff and all it's good for is to get you in trouble."

Rafe, Jr. emptied his cup in one gulp. That boy was going to have a bad drinking problem, one day.

Sula Jean was getting impatient. She was a Scorpio and would not be kept waiting.

"Did you come up here to drink that poison or to have one last big one with me?" she asked Rafe, Jr.

Rafe, Jr. got angry. Here was another person trying to tell him what to do and when. He grabbed Sula Jean by the shoulders and shook her.

"I'm sick of you!" he said. "I'm sick and Goddamn tired of everybody! Everybody! All I ever wanted to do was move to Memphis and make a dancing teacher at Arthur Murray and everybody's always got something else for me to do! I'm sick and tired of it!"

Rafe, Jr. turned up the bottle of Wild Turkey and took a long pull on it.

"Are you going to do me or not?" asked Sula Jean. "If you won't, they's plenty at the Owl in Memphis who will!"

Rafe, Jr. set the bottle down and had at Sula Jean. It was not easy because he was drunk.

"Let's go home," he said, later. "I've got to go to a party tonight. I've got to get home and get some sleep."

Sula Jean straightened her clothes and started down the hill to her car, walking behind Rafe, Jr. He got in the car, in the driver's seat.

"You can't drive!" said Sula Jean. "You're drunk! You're too drunk to drive!"

"I've got to drive!" said Rafe, Jr. "I'm too drunk to sing!"

That was a reference to an old joke he remembered from high school. No one else remembered it.

"I will not let you drive! This car is brand new! I ain't even made the first payment yet! Get out from behind that wheel!"

"I can too drive! It's just to my house, not a mile from here! If you don't want me to drive, you can just pull me out from behind this wheel! If you're big enough!"

"You damn bully! If you wreck this car, I'm taking it straight to your daddy!"

Rafe, Jr. started the engine and raced it in neutral until it was screaming. Then he engaged the gears and the little car shot away from the Barrow Pits, going a hundred miles an hour in seventy-five seconds.

When he got to the highway, Rafe, Jr. tried to slow down to make the turn, but he lost control and the Pimp swerved sharply, narrowly missed a big Buick driven by State Senator Oscar S. Baymule, then ran off the road into the side wall of a colored beer joint with "ITS A GO-GO GIRL IN HERE" painted on the front window.

The beer joint had no name. There had once been a sign on it, but someone had shot it off, years ago.

No one was hurt but the Pimp was destroyed. The fiberglass body was broken into a thousand shards and the frame was hopelessly bent.

Slowly, Rafe, Jr. and Sula Jean crawled out of the wreckage. Sula Jean saw what had happened to her car and started screaming. Rafe, Jr. leaned on the hood of a car that had just pulled up, and vomited.

State Senator Oscar S. Baymule, a temperance advocate, had turned back and stopped at the scene of the accident. He went up to Rafe, Jr., put hand on him and said, "I'm holding this man for the Law!"

Someone in the crowd pointed at Rafe, Jr. and said, "There's a boy needs put in the pen!"

An old colored man went in the GO-GO joint and telephoned Hazel Catfield, the town marshal.

A young man came up to Rafe, Jr. and grabbed him at the collar and twisted his shirt and pulled him up to his face and said, "I oughta whup yo' ass, buddy! You puked on my brother's Stingray!"

Senator Baymule pulled the two men apart. "Let the marshal handle this!" said the Senator. "I'm Senator Baymule! Do what I tell you! I'll see that this man is punished!"

Hazel Catfield, the town marshal, was a man, a big man, six-foot-five, with a massive overhanging gut. He was fifty-six in the waist and wore a size sixteen shoe. Sears did not stock his size in anything. Everything he wore had to be ordered out of the catalogue.

He had been in his office, a mile away, reading that month's issue of *Guns and Ammo*, when he got a telephone call from the colored man at the joint with no name.

"Come quick, Mr. Hazel! Boss Baymule is having trouble with Mr. Rafe, Jr. out at the joint with no name!"

State Senator Oscar S. Baymule was the political boss of Titus County and the man who had given Hazel Catfield his job as town marshal.

When Marshal Catfield heard that Boss Baymule was involved, he threw *Guns and Ammo* in the corner, grabbed his deputy, Burl Parsley — who was just leaving to eat pie *a la mode* at the Spit — and the two men raced out to the joint with no name in the official city car.

The first thing the marshal did when he got there was determine the *type* of problem Senator Baymule was having with Rafe, Jr.

"I make this out to be a traffic problem," he said, after he saw the wrecked Pimp.

He opened the trunk of the offical city car, picked around among some eighteen-by-twenty-four-inch signs there, found one that read:

CITY OF BLOAT
TRAFFIC ACCIDENT SQUAD

and slipped it into some grooves on the outside of the car door.

"Now, I'm ready to commence!" he said to the crowd.

Boss Baymule pointed to Rafe, Jr.

"Marshal," he said, "arrest that man!"

Sears did not stock anything in his size.

"Yes, sir, Mr. Baymule!"

The marshal handcuffed Rafe, Jr. to a signpost.

"What did he do, Mr. Baymule?" asked the marshal.

"Drunk! Driving drunk! Tried to run me off the road! Probably on dope!" said the Senator.

"Uh, oh!" said the marshal, and he went back to the trunk of the car, found a sign that read:

CITY OF BLOAT
ALCOHOL AND DRUG UNIT

and slipped it into the grooves on the outside of the car door.

The marshal looked at the Pimp, up close.

"That little car is flat totalled out," he said. "I mean, totalled!"

Sula Jean walked over to Rafe, Jr. handcuffed to the signpost, and slapped him a good one, right across the mouth.

"You can't slap a handcuffed prisoner!" said the marshal, grabbing her and holding her back. "That's *my* job!"

"That peckerwood raped me!" she said. "He took me back off up in them Barrow Pits and flat-out raped me! Threatened to kill me if I didn't give in!"

The marshal started writing this down on a tablet.

"Raped, you say?" he asked.

"Raped is right!" said Sula Jean.

Both of them pronounced the word "ripe," as in peaches when they get soft and fall off the tree.

"Used force, did he?" asked the marshal.

"What else can you call it when he held a broken beer bottle up to my throat?" asked Sula Jean.

The marshal turned to Rafe, Jr.

"Listen to me, Rafe, Jr.! Do you know what's going on here? Sula Jean is accusing you of raping her. That's life at Parchman Farm if you get convicted. But that ain't the worst. According to the Senator, here, you were doped up and drunk and driving that vehicle when it went out of control. You nearly ran into him and forced him off the road. That's ten years at Parchman, right there! But that still ain't the worst. The worst, I ain't even mentioned yet. You were driving that car. And that car is totalled out. Flat totalled out! A brand new car with factory air! Totalled out! That's enough to put you away for life, even without the rape charge! And you, fixing to get married to Davy Sue Merkle, come Saturday, a week!"

"This man ought to be put away for life, Marshal," said State Senator Oscar S. Baymule, "as an example to the other young people in this county — the greatest county in the great state of Mississippi!"

When Senator Baymule got wound up, there was no stopping him.

"I'll personally prosecute him!" he said. "I'll see that he does time!"

"I hope you get the chair, Rafe, Jr.!" said Sula Jean. "You raping peckerwood!"

"Rafe, Jr.," said the marshal, "I'm going to have to take you downtown."

Deputy Burl Parsley took Rafe, Jr. to jail in a private car. The marshal changed the sign on the city car to one that read:

CITY OF BLOAT
RAPE SQUAD

and he and Sula Jean drove back to the Barrow Pits to look at the scene of the crime.

"Up yonder is where it happened at," said Sula Jean, and she lead the marshal to the exact spot.

Hazel Catfield walked all over the area, picking up Seven-Up cans, paper cups, cigarette butts, putting them in envelopes and labeling them. He spotted something caught on a bush and quickly walked over to it. It was a cotton handkerchief. The marshal picked it up with a stick and called to Sula Jean. "This here will send that boy to the chair," he said.

"What is it?" asked Sula Jean.

"Evidence! See the initials 'RJ'? They stand for 'Rafe, Jr.'! This here is evidence!"

"What's so important about it?"

"This here han'chef has been used for soppin' a pecker!"

5

Rixie Leaptrot and Bunny Plan to Rob The Dog and Cat

Rixie Leaptrot and Bunny left the Spit Cafe as another ballad was being played on the juke box.

... soggy pretzels,
Lukewarm beer.
Oh why, oh why
Am I sitting here ... ?

The Bloat City Bench, a project of the Bloat Jaycees, stood on the sidewalk next door to the Spit, in front of the Chinaman's store, and they walked over to it. Before they could sit down, Bunny picked up the bench, one of those made of two-by-fours and poured concrete, and lifted it over his head, again and again. Mr. Ledbetter, the old farmer with the chickens, he in the bib overalls, saw the sight and was struck by it.

"What's that boy doing?" he asked.

"He likes to work out with the weights," said Rixie Leaptrot. He pronounced it "whytes."

There was still a crate of live chickens in the back of Mr. Ledbetter's truck.

"Them's mighty pretty chickens," said Rixie Leaptrot. "Rhode Island Reds?"

"They's Buffs," said the old farmer.

"Buff Orpingtons?"

The old farmer nodded.

"Mighty good eating!"

"Tough as wit leather!" said the old farmer. "I'm taking them into the Chinaman's store now. He's a'fixin' t'wring their necks for the Saturday trade."

Bunny picked up the bench with Rixie Leaptrot on it and lifted it over his head.

"Set me down and quit acting the fool!" said Rixie Leaptrot.

Bunny nodded and smiled brightly and put the bench back down on the ground.

"We gotta make plans, Bunny! We gotta figger out what to do! Where to go!"

They sat there on the bench nearly an hour while Rixie Leaptrot tried to decide.

"One thing we could do, that's to hitch a ride back over to Little Rock and stay at the Salvation Army for three days, or hitch on into Memphis. They got three places like the Salvation Army there, the Poplar Rescue Mission, the Baptist Mission and the St. Vincent DePaul Lodge. If a fella works it right, he can have nearly three weeks' room and board by going to first one, then the other, then start back again. In three weeks, something will turn up. Memphis. We better go on up to Memphis. We can't really go back to Arkansas, to Little Rock, not for a while, anyway. We just got run out of Arkansas! If they catch us back over there so soon, they might just take a notion to put us back on the road force."

Then Rixie Leaptrot noticed something. There was a line of people, all holding dogs on leashes, in front of a concrete block building down the street. Nearly fifty people, it was, all with dogs, all waiting to get in to the building.

"What's all them people with dogs?" asked Rixie Leaptrot of the farmer with the chickens.

"Dog doctor. Getting their shots. Today's the deadline! Get the shots and license renewed by today, or else tomorrow it's..." The old farmer made a hand like a pistol and put it up to his head. "Bang! Goodbye, doggie! I say, kill them all! I hate a barker. Give me a goat, any day! You can't beat a goat for a pet!"

After a while, Rixie Leaptrot said, "Bunny! That's it! There's our stake!"

Bunny smiled.

"Them people buying dog licenses are paying out cash money," said Rixie Leaptrot. "There must have been fifty of them in there since we been watching, since we been sitting here. Say each spins five dollars. Prolly, it's more! But just say each one spins five dollars! Say, five times thirty! That's a hundred and fifty dollars and I'll bet it's all in cash! A hundred and fifty dollars in cash, just waiting for us!"

Bunny smiled and nodded. He ran over to the old farmer's truck and picked a bale of hay out of the back and threw it up over his head, like it was a basketball.

The old farmer came out of the Chinaman's store, folding money, and saw Bunny and laughed and slapped his thigh.

"That's boy's a cutter! That's what he is! A cutter!"

He got in the cab of his truck, hid the chicken money up under the dashboard and drove away, toward home.

"I told you to quit acting the fool!" said Rixie Leaptrot to Bunny. "You throwing everything around like that and picking up cars, and one thing and another, that's gonna call people's attention to us, and that's no good if we're fixing to stick up the Dog and Cat!"

Bunny looked sheepish and hung his head.

"Now let's set back down here and wait for that crowd to thin out over there. The longer we wait, the more money's in the till."

Miss Effie Chad Reed took part-time work.

6

Miss Effie Chad Reed Takes Part-Time Work

Inside the small office of Dr. Reynaldo Quitman, D.V.M., sat Miss Effie Chad Reed, recently retired teacher of commercial subjects at Bloat High School, filling out dog license renewal forms. She wore glasses with thick lenses and was a little palsied.

Dr. Quitman had hired her part-time after she retired from the school system, to help her out. She had retired after forty-five years with the county and now drew Social Security income of one hundred seventy dollars a month and state teachers' retirement of fifty-six dollars and seventy-nine cents a month. Dr. Quitman paid her twenty dollars a week and vaccinated her cat free.

Miss Reed had worked all morning and was frazzled and nervous. Dr. Quitman had explained that this was the last day to renew licenses and that there would be a rush, that it would be their once-a-year busy spell, but she felt it was going to be more than she could take, even during the slow seasons, what with all the barking dogs that came in and out of there every day.

She hated barking dogs and several times in her life she had poisoned dogs in Bloat, but no one knew about it. She had never been caught or even suspected, and the city was a better place in which to live for what she had done.

Things slowed down for a moment, there were no more dogs in line, and she opened her purse and took out half an aspirin tablet and swallowed it with a sip of Coca-Cola from the vending machine in Dr. Quitman's office.

Yes, she had poisoned dogs and there were plenty of people she wished she could have poisoned, too. She could have poisoned ten or twelve people who had lived all their lives in Bloat, like she had, and it would have improved the city one hundred percent: Drinkers, smokers, fornicators, lewd women, people with defective mufflers on their cars. Yes, there was a lot she could do to tidy up Bloat, if she just wanted to. She might get rid of a few of the worst ones yet, in a year or two, before she was called up to Jesus, as sort of a parting gift to the city.

Miss Reed had never poisoned a cat. Not deliberately. Maybe a cat here and there had eaten a poisoned frankfurter she had set out for a dog and died as a result, but if so, it had been an accident and not her fault by any stretch of the imagination.

Lunch time. She had brought her lunch in a paper bag — a peanut butter sandwich, a stalk of celery and two devilled eggs. And coffee in a thermos bottle. Not *real* coffee. She had not been able to drink coffee for several years. It was the caffeine. It made her nervous and made her arms itch. She drank Postum or some other caffeine-free brand of coffee.

She chewed the peanut butter sandwich and thought about Sears Roebuck and Company. For forty years, she had been teaching Bloat girls how to work in offices and every last one of them, it seemed, had left town and gone up to Memphis, where they *had* offices, and got jobs. A lot of them, over the years, had wound up at Sears Roebuck and Company.

If she, Effie Chad Reed, had gone to work at Sears Roebuck and Company as soon as she got out of Blue Mountain College, back during the Depression, she would be retired today on profit-sharing and a good pension and not have to be working with dogs, things she had hated all her life, nor the likes of that Dr. Quitman, who was some kind of Cuban and always smelled like perfume.

7

Rixie Leaptrot and Bunny Stick Up The Dog and Cat

Rixie Leaptrot had been watching the Dog and Cat for over an hour and had decided to wait until the line of people with dogs was gone, then just walk in, he and Bunny, and take the money. The time finally arrived. It was late in the afternoon. There was no one in sight. The run of dogs was over.

"Come on, Bunny. Let's just walk in there and take the money! There's bound not to be no guard or watchman in a little place like that! All we'll have to do is scare them a good one!"

They walked across the street and into the building. There was no one there but a little old thin lady, who was wearing glasses with thick lenses and who had those brown "age" spots on her hands, the spots people get when they are in their seventies.

"What's your dog's name?" she asked. "I'll need it for the form."

"Name?" asked Rixie Leaptrot. He was thrown off by the old lady's request. It upset his rhythm.

The old lady had pulled a blank form out of a drawer, the application incidental to the renewal of a dog license, and was filling it in.

"What's his name? What kind is he? I need to know! Where is he? We can't give him a shot unless he's here. Any fool knows that!"

Miss Effie Chad Reed was thinking to herself that their dog was probably a barker who richly deserved one of her special frankfurters. The old man could use one of those frankfurters, too, thought Miss Reed. He was white trash, if she had ever seen it.

"What kind of dog is he? A bird dog? You look like bird hunters to me."

She sat there, pencil poised.

"We come for the money!" said Rixie Leaptrot.

"I NEED TO KNOW THE DOG'S NAME! YOU'LL HAVE TO SPEAK UP! I'M DEAF! I CAN'T HEAR A THING IF YOU SPEAK LOW!"

"WE COME FOR THE MONEY! GIVE US THE DOG MONEY AND THEY WON'T BE NO TROUBLE!"

"I HEARD THAT! ARE YOU TRYING TO ROB ME?"

"GIVE US THE MONEY, I SAID, AND I MEAN IT! IF YOU DON'T 'FORE LONG GIVE US THE MONEY, I'M GONNA HAVE MY HELPER PICK YOU UP!"

Rixie Leaptrot turned to Bunny and said, "If I'd a'known they was an old person in here, I would have skipped this job. You never want to try to rob an old person, Bunny. They're all just as mule-headed as they can be! They just won't shell out! You never want any old people on a jury, either. I can tell you that."

Rixie Leaptrot turned to the old lady. "I'VE GIVE YOU ALL THE TIME I'M GONNA!"

"YOU CAN'T HAVE THE MONEY! IT'S DR. QUITMAN'S MONEY!"

"Pick her up, Bunny. Hold her high! Twirl her, if you have to, 'til she jars loose with the money."

Bunny picked up Miss Reed and held her over his head.

She screamed. "HELP! POLICE! BLOODY MURDER!"

Bunny was getting ready to twirl her like a baton when the door to the office opened and Marshal Hazel Catfield entered, leading three German shepherds, two Dobermans and a blooded possum-charger on leashes.

"Is it too late to get the city dogs vaccinated? Say, what's going on here?"

"Marshal, they tried to get the dog money! He's fixing to twirl me until I pay it over!"

Marshal Catfield took Rixie Leaptrot and Bunny in charge. "This ain't just robbery, buddy pals," he said. "You trying to take that dog money amounts to stealing city funds, and that's big trouble. You boys are in for it now. Chances are, you'll get ten to twelve, if you're lucky."

"Ten to twelve," repeated Rixie Leaptrot. "You hear that, Bunny? Ten to twelve! That's the big time! Dadburn! Ten to twelve! Well, a man has to play out his string."

Miss Reed pointed at Rixie Leaptrot. "I knew you'd come to this! I remember you from the tenth grade! You were always drumming on your desk!"

The marshal put the two men in the back seat of the city car and handcuffed them together, then he opened the trunk and looked among the signs until he found one that read:

CITY OF BLOAT
ARMED ROBBERY SQUAD

and slipped it in the grooves on the front door of the car.

"Yes sir," he said, "ten to twelve at Parchman Farm."

Bunny took the chain between the handcuffs in his fingers and pinched it in two.

The city car pulled up to the Bloat jail, a two-story concrete block building.

"Sure hate to tie up the cell with prisoners," said the marshal. "The Methodist Church Young People, they roller skates in there every Friday night, when they ain't no prisoners. Smoothest concrete floor in the whole county! Yes sir, I love young people!"

"I hate them!" said Rixie. "That's the normal thing, to hate them!"

Bunny held up his free arm and showed the marshal the broken chain on the handcuffs. He smiled, broadly.

"Now how in the world did that happen?" asked the marshal, scratching his head.

"Them arns just musta give," explained Rixie.

The marshal unlocked the heavy steel-barred cell door and shut the two men away. The cell was large, dark and cool. The floor had been mopped with a rich pine tar solution, which stung the eyes. There was one other prisoner.

In a corner, passed out drunk on the floor, lying in a pool of his own vomit, was Rafe, Jr. His clothes were a mess. His dark coat was ripped down the back, his dark pants were torn at the knees, his Italian shoes were muddy and his four-foot-long key chain was broken.

"That's that unhappy rich kid we saw in the Spit Cafe, Bunny!" said Rixie Leaptrot. "The one's fixing to get married, come Saturday a week."

Bunny smiled and looked for something to lift. Since everything else was fastened down, he picked up Rafe, Jr. and twirled him over his head.

"Put that boy down, Bunny!" said Rixie Leaptrot. "He's sicker'n a dog, as it is!"

Rixie Leaptrot and Bunny sat there for three hours. It was getting dark outside.

Once or twice, Rafe, Jr. stirred, then groaned.

Davy Sue had an Arkansas face – the face that won the West.

8

Enter Davy Sue Merkle and Rafe Munger, Land Deals

It was getting along about eight-thirty in the evening when there was a commotion in the room outside the jail cell, after which the door to the cell block opened and the marshal entered, followed by a determined young woman and an older man who looked important.

The woman was under twenty, maybe under eighteen, and was four and a half feet tall, without a curve on her. She had long carrot-colored hair, pulled back behind her head and held there by a rubber band, and was wearing a tight-fitting pair of pale blue shorts and a white halter. She was barefooted, and had what is known to science as an Arkansas face — the face that won the West.

She was the bride-to-be.

"Rafe, Jr., get up off that floor and come over here to me!" she ordered. "Get up this minute! I hate you! You've just ruined everything! Get up and talk to me! You hear me! Get up right now!"

She pounded on the bars of the cell with tiny fists and kicked at them with her bare foot.

Rafe, Jr. turned over, and with his face toward the bars,

vomited again.

"Look at him!" screamed Davy Sue. "He's puking at me!"

"Let me in there, Hazel," said the important-looking man. "Let me talk to my son."

"Well, all right, Mr. Big Rafe," said the marshal. "Seeing it's you."

Rafe Munger was a big man. He wore a heavy brown suit, which was too tight for him, and brown wingtip shoes that had just been polished down at the barber's. The black paint on the edges of the soles was still wet and picking up lint. Big Rafe had a fat, fleshy face, almost a true purple in color. People meeting him for the first time always wanted to loosen his collar.

Hazel Catfield unlocked the cell door and Big Rafe entered, walked slowly over to Rafe, Jr. and stood there a minute looking down at him, on the floor.

"I ought to kick you right smack in the slats," he said.

"Don't kill me, Poppa Loppa!"

"That's just what I feel like doing! Look at you! Drunk! Drunk and running with a tramp!"

"I'm sorry, Poppa Loppa!"

"Do you know what kind of mess you're in? Foon with that girl! They can put you away for life! They can give you the chair! My money can't save you this time!"

"He'll get twenty to thirty, for sure, Mr. Big Rafe," said Marshal Hazel Catfield.

"See there! Twenty to thirty, for sure!" bellowed Big Rafe.

"I'm sorry, Poppa Loppa!"

"After all I've done for you! All that education I bought you!"

"I'm sorry, Poppa Loppa!"

"Didn't I send you through Ole Miss?"

"You did that, Poppa Loppa! You sure enough did that!"

"And didn't you make Mr. Popularity?"

"I was put up for it, Poppa Loppa. I made Mr. Reb!"

"Mr. Reb, and look at you now!"

"I'm sorry, Poppa Loppa!"

"Do you understand that everything is ruined, because of you? Ruined! They can't be no wedding now, thanks to you! No wedding! Do you get that?"

"No wedding?" screeched Davy Sue.

"No wedding!" repeated Big Rafe.

"But the invitations is already out!" said Davy Sue. "The cake is already ordered! A four-dollar cake! Just gotta be throwed away!"

"I'll pay for the cake, Davy Sue," said Rafe, Jr.

"To Hell with the cake!" said Big Rafe. "That ain't the worst part, the cake! Do you know what the worst part is? The Executive

Big Rafe had a fat, fleshy face, almost a true purple in color.

Vice-President of all the Roller Board Roadside Inns is coming down here from Memphis, and maybe the Vice-President for High Rises, right along with him, just for the wedding, all because I'm trying to swing a Roller Board Roadside Inn out at the Cloverleaf."

"I didn't know that, Poppa Loppa."

"They're coming! It's on their date book!"

"I'm sorry, Poppa Loppa!"

"Now, I've got to call them and say it's off, because my son's been foon with a girl!"

"I'm sorry, Poppa Loppa!"

"What am I supposed to tell them! That at age sixty-one, I wound up being a raper's father?"

"I'll make it up to you, Poppa Loppa. Honest I will!"

"How you gonna make up anything? You're gonna be on the inside, doing twenty to thirty!"

Big Rafe strode back over to the bars and beat his head against them.

"Don't take on like that, Mr. Big Rafe," said the marshal. "If he's lucky, he'll get out in ten to twelve."

Davy Sue started crying.

"Hazel," asked Big Rafe, "is there no possibility he could be turned loose just to get married, then brought right back here, on my honor?"

"There ain't a chance in the world," said the marshal. "If it was just ordinary foon with a girl, I could let him out, right now. But this is more than that. He almost run down Senator Baymule! Drunk driving! He totalled out that girl's sporty little Pimp, with mag wheels and factory air, and most near killed the political boss of Titus County! Now, that's trouble! No sir, there's no chance of him getting out, not with the senator telling me to keep him here 'til he rots!"

Big Rafe started sobbing. Davy Sue kept on sobbing, only louder.

Rixie Leaptrot, who had been taking all of this in, got up and walked over to Big Rafe.

"Maybe *I* can think of a way out," he said, putting an arm around Big Rafe's shoulder.

"You? Who are you?" asked Big Rafe.

"Them's the ones tried to stick up the Dog and Cat," said the marshal. "They'll get ten to twelve, for sure."

"I'm Rixie Leaptrot. My folks was circus people. I've smoked ready-rolled cigarettes since I was six and I know three people in books."

"What can you do?" asked Big Rafe.

"See that boy over there?" asked Rixie Leaptrot, pointing to

Bunny. "His name is Bunny Whitesides and he's one of the best-looking young men east of the Wabbaseka Scatters. Clean-living, healthy, pure in heart. I'd ask him to lift you but this ain't the time or place."

"What are you getting at?" asked Big Rafe.

"A proxy. I know enough about the law to know a fella can get married by proxy. Bunny can be a proxy for your son! You can put it out that your son got sick, sudden, or that he got called up by the Reserves, overnight."

"A proxy?" mused Big Rafe. "A proxy wedding!"

"A proxy wedding is legal, just as binding as any. Just get holt of your lawyer and have him draw up the papers. After the wedding, you can go to work to get your boy off. If you do, he'll be married to that little lady, yonder, and can set up house just like nothing ever happened."

"What if I can't get him off!" asked Big Rafe.

"If you can't, he'll still be married anyway, and can go to the pen dreaming of his sweet bride and her charms."

"You're talking dirty, mister!" said Davy Sue.

"Shut up, girl," said Big Rafe.

"You shut YOUR mouth, Big Rafe!" said Davy Sue. "If you think you're gonna push me around, you got another think coming! I'm fixing to be your wedded daughter-in-law so you remember that and stop treating me like I was some little girl clerking in bin goods at the Salvation Army store!"

"I'm sorry, Davy Sue," said Big Rafe. "Let's listen to this man. I think he's got an idea."

"It's a good idea," said Rixie Leaptrot, "but they's strings on it!"

"What kind of strings?" asked Big Rafe.

"Me and Bunny, here, we're in jail right now all because of a little misunderstanding. Bunny was just demonstrating his strong-man act for that old lady at the Dog and Cat when she got the damn-fool notion we was trying to hold her up."

"What's this got to with that boy being my son's proxy?"

"Just this: If you can't get us out of here, get the charges dismissed, we ain't interested."

"What about that, Hazel?" asked Big Rafe.

"You say it's a mistake?" asked the marshal. "You mean you weren't trying to rob the Dog and Cat?"

"No sirree!" said Rixie Leaptrot."I can't for the life of me understand how that old lady took the notion we was trying to rob her."

"How about it, Hazel?" asked Big Rafe. "Can't you dismiss the charges?"

The marshal pondered.

"I reckon. If it was just a mistake. I can do it. Their names ain't gone down in the jail book yet."

Big Rafe extended his right hand to Rixie Leaptrot.

"Mister, I'm going to step down the street and talk to my lawyer. If he's says it's OK, then you got a deal!"

9

Big Rafe Wakes Up His Lawyer

Swan Bagley, Attorney at Law and Notary Public, was asleep on the sofa in his living room when Big Rafe rang his door bell.

"Swan, I hate to bust up your nap," said Big Rafe, "but I got a problem. My boy, Rafe, Jr., he's done another damn-fool thing. They got him down in jail on a rape charge. Sula Measles, she claimed he raped her. Hell, we both know better than that! They got him on drunk driving, too. Totalled out a new Pimp. Almost hit Senator Baymule. Oscar, he's mad! He's making the marshal hold Rafe, Jr. in jail. You can't hardly blame Oscar, since it *was* his daughter Rafe, Jr. cut up with that beer bottle, a time or two back.

"Anyway, Rafe, Jr. is supposed to get married a week from tomorrow to Davy Sue Merkle. Hell, I guess you know that! The wedding's all been scheduled. Announcements out, pictures sent to the *Commercial Appeal*. Cake already ordered.

"Biggest thing is the Roller Board Roadside Inn deal I'm putting together. Vice-President of Roller Board is coming down here for the wedding. Maybe a couple of others, too. The Roller Board men are expecting a wedding, but we can't have a wedding if the groom is in jail."

Swan Bagley raised his hand. "You could hold the wedding in

the jail house. Have the bride and groom hold hands through the bars. I'll get a court order."

"Don't talk silly, Swan," said Big Rafe. "That'd be the worst thing we could do! Listen here, Swan, I don't need to tell you, I'm working this Roller Board Roadside Inn deal awful close to the bone. I've signed a contract with the Stucco brothers to buy one hundred acres of land from them out at the Cloverleaf and given them a personal check for twenty-five thousand dollars as earnest money. I told them I had a Roller Board franchise. I had to, or else they wouldn't have taken my check for that much money."

"You mean you don't have the franchise?" asked Swan Bagley. "I thought you had it in the bag."

"It ain't definite, Swan. I'm supposed to go to Memphis Monday and give them some more financial statements. I'm sure I'll get it, and when I do, when it's in the bag, I can borrow big money on it. I can get a loan from any bank in Memphis, any bank, or CIT, or Associates, anybody, to build the motel and make that check I gave the Stucco brothers good."

"Good?" asked Swan Bagley. "You mean you gave a bad check as earnest money?"

"I had to, Swan. They was no other way I could swing it. The Stucco brothers, they don't know it's bad, yet. They're holding it, until I say deposit it."

Swan Bagley shook his head from side to side. "Sounds like fraud, to me," he said.

"I'm skating on thin ice, all the way," said Big Rafe. "If I don't get that franchise, and don't get to borrow the money, then, Swan, I'm in trouble. The Stucco brothers will hold me to that contract. They will! You know a Dago!"

Swan Bagley folded his hands and walked around his living room a few times.

"What I don't understand," he said, "is, what's the Roller Board deal got to do with the wedding?"

"Everything! If word got out up at Roller Board home office that I had a son in jail for rape, then they'd drop me like a hot potato!"

"As I see it, then, you've got to have a wedding, just to keep things respectable with Roller Board's home office, just so there won't be any complications about the franchise. Am I right, so far?"

"And we gotta keep it a secret that Rafe, Jr. is in jail. Right, Swan! Dead right!"

"We've got to have a wedding, but your groom is in jail and Senator Oscar S. Baymule is making sure he stays there. Oscar is vindictive. He'll stick it to your boy. Five to ten years, I'd guess."

Big Rafe hung his head. "It's been coming to that, anyway,

since he was ten years old and set fire to all those new Pontiacs down at the Motorama," he said.

Swan Bagley put his hand on Big Rafe's shoulder. "Rafe, now don't misunderstand me, but why is it that Davy Sue would still want to marry Rafe, Jr.?"

"That Davy Sue, she's got a head on her! It was her that put it in my mind to work out this Roller Board deal. That girl is smart! I want her in the family. She's going to make us all rich!"

"She wants to go ahead with the wedding, then?" asked Swan Bagley.

"She knows what she's getting into. She know's Rafe, Jr. is not perfect."

Attorney Swan Bagley reached a decision. "Taking everything into account, then, we've got to have a wedding!" he said.

"What about a proxy?" asked Big Rafe. "There's a fellow here in town, a fraternity brother of Rafe, Jr.'s. He's willing to act as proxy. That's what I'm here for, to see if a proxy wedding is legal, all that sort of thing. With this boy acting as a proxy, I can put it out that Rafe, Jr. is sick to death up in the Baptist Hospital in Memphis, or that he got called up by the National Guard."

"National Guard?" asked Swan Bagley. "I thought he got a dishonorable discharge from the National Guard."

"That he did! But not everybody knows it. It'll work. I'll tell everybody he's been called up by the National Guard for a special assignment. Maybe overseas."

"A proxy is legal," said Swan Bagley, "provided the right papers are drawn up. Signed by the parties. Notarized. It'll cost you. At least twenty-five, thirty dollars."

"Money's no object!" said Big Rafe. "Draw up the papers!"

"Who's the proxy? I'll need his name."

"Bunny something. I'll bring him down here and he can tell you himself."

"Will Rafe, Jr. sign? He'll have to sign before a notary or it's not legal."

"He'll sign."

"That boy's got a trial coming up," said Swan Bagley. "It'll be a big help to him if he's a new bridegroom. Davy Sue is well liked around here. It'll be to his advantage to have her sitting in the courtroom, praying for him. You might point that out to him if he's the leastways uneasy about going ahead with the wedding."

"He'll see it that way, too. I promise."

"He'll have it easier with a jury, the way I see it, if Davy Sue's his bride."

"I'll get the proxy down here right now. You can start drawing up the papers."

"What's the hurry? Can't it wait until morning?"

"A man ought never to waste time. That's what Davy Sue says. That's how she was able to finish high in three years. Going in the summers. No sir! A man should not waste time!"

Big Rafe hurried back to the jail and gathered all the parties around him.

"You got a deal, mister," he said to Rixie Leaptrot. "As soon as the marshal turns you loose, I'll get you and Bunny fixed up with a room, some new clothes, a little money, all that."

"You hear that, Bunny?" said Rixie Leaptrot. "We struck it rich! We're fixing to get a new suit of clothes and some walking-around money!"

Bunny smiled.

Big Rafe extended his hand, first to Rixie Leaptrot, then to Bunny. "It's a deal, then," he said. "We got a regular bidnessman's deal!"

"Solomn deal," agreed Rixie Leaptrot. Bunny nodded his approval.

They walked out of the jail, Big Rafe, Rixie Leaptrot, Bunny and Davy Sue, leaving Rafe, Jr. lying on the floor with bad cramps in his stomach.

Davy Sue walked beside Rixie Leaptrot. "That Bunny is sure one fine-looking fella," she said to him.

"He is that! His heart's in the right place, too! He's as decent as they come!"

Bunny heard Davy Sue talking about him and picked her up and held her over his head, then started throwing her up, way, way up and catching her gently as she came down.

"Oh, Glory!" she screamed from on high. "Oh, Bunny!"

Bunny set her on the ground and smiled at her.

"Bunny, I got a notion you might try to pull me on a couch!" she said.

Big Rafe and Davy Sue led Rixie Leaptrot and Bunny to Mumm's Dollar Store, where Big Rafe bought them each a new dress suit of clothes: double-knit powder blue slacks with bell-bottoms, navy blue herringbone double-knit sport coats with padded shoulders and a box back, double-knit shirts, red plastic belts, double-knit knit ties and red crinkle plastic slip-on shoes, with a gold chain across each vamp.

At Big Rafe's insistence, the two men changed into their new clothes right there in the back of the store, in Mumm's stockroom, among some crates of plastic flowers and boxes of straw raincoats made in Hong Kong.

Once they were presentable, Big Rafe took them across town, with Davy Sue still in tow, to meet attorney Swan Bagley.

The proxy and his friend, Rixie Leaptrot.

"The leading case on proxy wedding is Nail vs. Gebauer, 15 Mississippi Appeals, 147," said Swan Bagley, who had been researching the law since Big Rafe had left to retrieve his proxy.

"There was fraud in the inducement, in that case," he said. "Nothing like that here, that I can see."

"Everything's on the up and up, Swan," said Big Rafe.

With that, Swan Bagley took down the information he needed and drew up the proxy agreement.

"If I were you, Rafe," said Swan Bagley, "I'd wait until tomorrow to get it signed, when Rafe, Jr. is feeling better and knows what he's doing."

"Whatever you say, Swan," said Big Rafe.

Davy Sue went on home, leaving Big Rafe standing in the street with Rixie Leaptrot and Bunny.

"You boys will need to clean up and get a good night's sleep," said Big Rafe. "Here's fifty dollars. Go down yonder and get a room at the Mink Motel. Tell Coy Mink you'll be there a week or ten days. Tell him to put it down to me."

"Whatever you say," said Rixie Leaptrot, taking the money.

"I'll get with you in the morning and we can go over our story," said Big Rafe. "Say, that reminds me, I'd better get down to the *Tomcat* office and find out what they've heard about all this!"

"If they got the story, you better try to kill it," said Rixie Leaptrot.

"I'll talk to Tubby Turmath. It won't be any trouble."

Big Rafe left for the *Tomcat* office and Rixie Leaptrot and Bunny entered the Mink Motel and approached the registration desk. There was a fat young man sitting there. He wore a black suit, white shirt and black tie. His hair was parted in the middle of his head and there was a strange look in his black, little pig eyes.

"A room for the next week or ten days," said Rixie Leaptrot. "And put it down to Rafe Munger. Mr. Big Rafe."

The young man did not move. He did not say anything, either. He just looked at Rixie Leaptrot with those strange, black, little pig eyes.

"We want a room for the next week or ten days," repeated Rixie Leaptrot.

"I moan' a kill you!" said the desk clerk.

"What's that?" asked Rixie Leaptrot.

At that moment, a man, some years older than the desk clerk, appeared from someplace in the back.

"Now, Coy, none of that, son," he said to the clerk.

"What's the matter with that boy?" demanded Rixie Leaptrot.

"Sorry," said the older man. "He's not feeling well, right along in here." He pointed to his head. "He's taking treatments."

Rixie Leaptrot and Bunny were shown to a room with standard twin beds, coat hangers, luggage rack, sterilized toilet seat and a Bible. Bunny danced around the room with happiness. It was the most elegant he had ever been in in his life. He picked up some furniture and held it over his head. It was made of cheap plywood and masonite, motel issue, boxboard — no challenge for Bunny's strength.

"Set down that chester drawers!" said Rixie Leaptrot. "Let's get some sleep! We've had one busy day!"

Mrs. Tait Tate bought him for a bad dog.

10

Duane Yancey Takes A Room At Mrs. Tait Tate's

Mrs. Tait Tate lived in a large, white, wooden Victorian home, with two stories and a floored attic, about five blocks off Main Street, at the southernmost edge of Bloat. The house was set back on three acres of land.

Mrs. Tate, herself, answered the door when Yancey knocked.

She was an average size woman, a little on the heavy side, in her late sixties. She was wearing a flowered-print dress, with a white muslin apron over it, and a man's pair of maroon and gold carpet slippers.

"Yes?" she said, when she saw Yancey.

"Mrs. Tate?"

"Yes?"

"I work for the *Tomcat*. Mr. Turmath said I might be able to rent a room here."

"You want to rent a room?"

"Yes, ma'am."

Mrs. Tate let Yancey into the house and led him down the hall to the back and showed him a large, cool room with a lot of good furniture in it.

"Ten dollars a week," she said.

"I'll take it," said Yancey.

"Before you can move in, I'll need to ask you some questions. I never saw you before. You're not a local boy. You may have come here planning to get my breath while I'm asleep ..."

"Aw ma'am, you don't need to worry about anything like that. I'm just a reporter for the *Tomcat*. Mr. Turmath told me you rented rooms ..."

"Don't move," whispered Mrs. Tate, freezing. "Hold real still. Hold real still and he won't jump you."

"Jump me?" asked Yancey.

"The dog. He's right behind you. He don't know you. That's all. He's just uncertain."

Mrs. Tate moved away from her chair slowly, toward the open door behind Yancey. There in the doorway, a very large German shepherd dog was crouched, ready to spring. She moved slowly toward the dog and slowly reached out her arm to the door and shut it slowly as the dog began to growl, deep within his bowels. She continued to slowly shut the door until it was a foot away from the jamb; then she shut it very fast and clicked the lock. The dog let out a fierce, frustrated growl of rage, ran down the hall, pushed open the front door, ran out to Yancey's car, grabbed the front bumper in his teeth and shook it vigorously. Yancey and Mrs. Tate watched him through the window in the living room.

"I bought him for a bad dog," she said.

"How bad is he? He looks dangerous to me!"

"A woman living alone needs protection. I read about all that killing and raping and knocking in the head in Memphis. I read every word. It's just a matter of time until it spreads down here to Bloat. When it gets here, that dog will take care of it."

"He looks dangerous to me!"

"He was in the army. He's an old army dog."

"I say he's too dangerous. How am I going to get in my car?"

"I'll call him off and lock him in the hall."

"I don't know about renting a room here, with that dog. I'm afraid he might jump me if I were to come in late some night."

"I don't allow nobody here to keep late hours. Are you a Christian?"

"I guess so."

"You guess so! When the Lord comes, he'll want to know definite!"

"Is there anyone else in Bloat who rents rooms?"

"Just me. Most people are glad to rent here, in a Christian home where they'll be safe."

Mrs. Tate had attachments on every door and window in the house that played music-box tunes every time one of them was opened. She also had some kind of electrical device that switched the floor lamps on and off, all over the house, all night long, to make burglars outside think there were people up and moving around inside. At intervals during the night, a tape recording of the voices of loud, rough men was played through a loudspeaker under the eaves on the second floor of the house.

"I believe there's a burglar in the yard, Spike!"

"Let me at him," replied a gravelly voice. "I'll get hold of him and make him sorry he tried to rob this house!"

"Better take this axe with you!"

Then there would follow the sound of police whistles and gunshots, all taped and played through the loudspeaker.

"I guess I'll take the room," said Yancey. He was getting tired and Tubby Turmath had ordered him to return at once to the *Tomcat* office and help get out the next day's edition.

"You say you're a Christian?"

"Yes, ma'am."

"Church of Christ?"

"Uh ... Methodist."

"Methodist? I won't allow cigar smoking in my house!"

"No, ma'am."

"All right. You can move in."

Yancey paid Mrs. Tate ten dollars, a week's rent, and she went outside and locked the dog in a shed until Yancey could get his luggage in the house.

After changing his clothes, Yancey reported back to the *Tomcat* office and relieved Davy Sue's brother Frank, who went home for supper. Yancey was alone in the office, writing up a notice of a De Molay pie supper, when the telephone rang.

"*Tomcat* office," he answered.

A colored man's voice on the other end of the line said, "Rafe, Jr. was arrested this afternoon for rape."

"Rafe, who?" asked Yancey.

"Rafe Junior Munger. He was arrested this afternoon for rape. Wrecked a car and puked on a Stingray. He's in jail right now. This is a friend."

The voice hung up. It had been the owner of the beer joint with no name calling, the one whose place had been rammed by Rafe, Jr. in the Pimp. Big Rafe had refused to stand good for the repairs. Big Rafe had told the owner he could sue him if he did not like it.

Yancey telephoned the jail and Marshal Hazel Catfield answered.

"This is Duane Yancey down at the *Tomcat*. I hear you got Rafe Junior Munger in there."

The marshal assumed the story was out and told all.

"How do you spell your name, marshal? I want to make sure I get it right in the *Tomcat*."

Hazel Catfield had never had his name in the *Tomcat* and was thrilled by the prospect. "You going to put my name in the paper?"

"Yes sir!"

"That'll be mighty nice!"

"Do I have all the facts, now, before I hang up?"

"Well, sir, like I said, we've got evidence enough to send Rafe, Jr. to Parchman for life. It was one of the most awful crimes in the history of this county. I've been marshal for twenty years and I've seen some bad men in my day, but never nothing like Rafe, Jr.!

"We found three hundred thousand dollars' worth of hard drugs under the back seat of his car," said the marshal, beginning to get carried away. "We figger the Mafia's in on it and that Rafe, Jr. was fixing to take that girl across a state line as part of an interstate call-girl ring."

The marshal was really wound up and talked on for another ten minutes, throwing in charges of arson, damage to real property, suspected buggery, and hints of connections with several unsolved murders.

"Thanks, marshal," said Yancey.

"My pleasure. Be sure now you spell my name right. It's CATFIELD. Lot of times, people think it's HATFIELD. It's CATFIELD. C-A-T. CATFIELD."

"Yes sir! I got it!" said Yancey.

Yancey wrote two thousand words on the Rafe, Jr. story, full of the colorful details given him by the marshal, and set it up for the front page under the headline:

RAFE MUNGER, JR. HELD ON RAPE, DOPE,
DRUNK CHARGES. MURDER LINK SUSPECTED.
FACES LIFE AT PARCHMAN.
SPORTY PIMP TOTALLED.

and put it in the copy basket on Tubby Turmath's desk.

Tubby Turmath returned from the Country Club about eight-thirty p.m. Friday night and started looking through the stories on his desk. When he saw the story about Rafe, Jr., he yelled to Yancey.

"Hey, Weak-Eyes! Get your butt in here!"

"Yes sir, Mr. Turmath?"

"Where'd you get all this stuff about Rafe, Jr.?"

"Checked it out after I got a tip on the phone."

"Boy — Weak-Eyes — We can't run nothing like this, even if it's true. We'd get our ass sued off if we was to run this . . ."

At that moment, Big Rafe walked in the *Tomcat* office, tired and played out after his busy and unpleasant day. He had one final mission to accomplish before he could go home and to bed. He had to be sure there would be nothing in the *Tomcat* about Rafe, Jr.'s troubles.

Tubby Turmath and his wife, Mona Mutt Turmath, were partners with Big Rafe, along with Dr. Dennis Dennis, the dentist, and his wife, Baxter Dennis, in the company that was trying to get the Roller Board Roadside Inn franchise.

"Tubby, can I see you alone?" asked Big Rafe.

"Weak-Eyes, get your butt on out of here, so's we can talk bidness."

Big Rafe shut the door to Tubby's office behind Yancey as he left.

"Tubby, I need a favor," he said. "It's a favor for me, but it's in your own interest, as well. Rafe, Jr. did a damn-fool thing this afternoon. Out foon with that Sula Measles. Wrecked her car. Drunk. You know Rafe, Jr."

"You want it kept out of the *Tomcat*?" asked Tubby.

"Not just for me, Tubby. For you and Mona, as well."

"I gottcha!"

"You and Mona have just as big an interest in this as I have. If it was to get out that my boy was no-count, if it was to get back to Roller Board's home office that he's had the past he's had, it would mean the end of any franchise down at the Cloverleaf."

"Sure would at that!" said Tubby. "Sure as Hell would!"

"So, if you could keep it out of the *Tomcat*, you see, we'd both stand to gain."

"I gottcha! Sure, we'll keep it out. That's what owning a paper is for!"

"There's another thing, Tubby. It was Oscar Baymule that Rafe, Jr. almost ran off the road. Oscar, he's vindictive. He's going to prosecute Rafe, Jr. hisself. He's fixed it where I can't get him out on bail. That means he's going to be smackdab in jail when it's time for his wedding."

"Won't even let a man out of jail to get married!"

"No sir! Rafe, Jr. is liable to be in jail for months. And we've got to account for him when it comes time for that wedding. I've talked to Swan Bagley. We agreed to let it out that Rafe, Jr. got called up by the National Guard —"

"I thought he was thrown out of the guard," said Tubby.

"He was, but not everybody knows it. I'm telling it around that he got called up, just one man, because of some special skills, and that he will be on active duty indefinitely. That way, we can get through the wedding easy enough."

"Get through the wedding? How, with Rafe, Jr. in jail?"

"A proxy. One of Rafe, Jr.'s frat brothers from Ole Miss is in town. He's going to act as proxy for Rafe, Jr. The agreement has already been drawn up."

"What do you want me to do?" asked Tubby.

"Run a little piece in the *Tomcat* about Rafe, Jr. being called up."

"Glad to," said Tubby. "I'll mention about the proxy, too. What's his name?"

"Er, I don't know for sure. They call him 'Bunny.' I'll get back to you with it, if you need it."

"We don't need it. Don't need it at all."

"Thanks, Tubby. We'll both gain out of this. When that motel gets going, we'll be making money hand over fist."

Tubby laughed his idiot laugh. "Hand over fist! That's a good one!"

After Big Rafe left, Tubby Turmath picked up the story written by Duane Yancey and re-read it.

"Weak-Eyes! Get your butt in here!"

"Yes sir!"

"Take this story and tear it up! We don't print stuff like that! Lies, hearsay! Tear it up!"

Yancey looked disappointed.

"Get your butt back in there at your desk and write up a story about that same boy, Rafe, Jr., being called up by the National Guard. Emergency. Special duty. Special training. Be gone for months. Say he was sent to Iceland. Say there's going to be a frat brother of his from Ole Miss to act as his proxy at his wedding to Miss Davy Sue Merkle, come Saturday a week."

Duane Yancey went back to his desk and wrote that story. It was just a paragraph. He sent it back to the printers, to be set up for the next day's issue.

11

Duane Yancey Wakes the Town

It was ten o'clock at night and the next day's issue of the *Tomcat* was at press. Duane Yancey and Frank Merkle, Davy Sue's brother, were sitting in the lobby of Mutt Brothers Funeral Home, drinking Cokes. Nothing in Bloat except the funeral home was open at ten o'clock at night. Not even the Spit. If you wanted a Coke, you had to get it out of the machine at Mutt Brothers. The funeral home stayed open twenty-four hours because there was never any telling when someone would take a notion to view remains.

"You ever think," asked Frank, "that right in the next room, they's dead people?"

"I guess I hadn't thought about it," said Yancey.

"Always one or two dead people."

"I hadn't realized it," said Yancey. "That there were dead people here, I mean."

"And us, sitting out here, sipping Co-Cola, like it was nothing."

Yancey shivered a little.

"It makes you tough, working for a paper," said Frank.

Yancey finished his Coke, said goodnight to Frank and got in his car and drove to his new home, Mrs. Tate's rooming house. It was dark as he approached, but when he was twenty yards away, some lights went on in the front yard and he heard voices, like grizzly merchant seamen quarreling.

"There's someone sneaking around out back!"

"It must be a burglar! Let's go get him!"

"Bust his head! Let the dog at him!"

Then there were the sounds of fierce dogs growling and grown men screaming and villains being clubbed into insensibility.

Suddenly, the lights went out and the voices were silent and everything was quiet. Yancey did not know what to make of it all. He waited a while in his car, then got out and walked up to the house.

Lodgers on the ground floor could be heard snoring through the open windows. Yancey tried to open the front door. It was locked and Mrs. Tate had not given him a key.

How to get in? Mrs. Tate had warned him about late hours. It would only make her angry to awaken her. Best he try to get in a window.

He walked around back of the house and tried the screen on one of the windows in his room. It was loose. It would be easy to remove. He shook it gently. It was coming off the window easily, when the electric burglar alarm sounded.

Sirens, gongs, searchlights, steam whistles! Mercury vapor lights went on, all over the property! Mrs. Tate's dog, driven insane by the clamor, lunged at Yancey through the window of his own bedroom and got tangled in the screen.

Yancey ran to his car and got in and locked the door seconds before the dog arrived, dragging the screen with him. The other lodgers turned on their lights and stood in their rooms, shivering, expecting to die at the hands of cut-throats.

When he saw the lights in the house, the dog turned away from the car and ran toward them, saliva dripping from his jowls, on the attack, insane with rage, because if there was one thing he hated, it was sudden bright lights at night.

Mrs. Tate came out on the porch and fired a shotgun in the air. "You'll have to kill me before you can have my body!" she screamed at the imaginary villains in the darkness.

A man down the road telephoned for Marshal Hazel Catfield. In ten minutes he arrived on the scene, disarmed Mrs. Tate and settled things down in the house. Then he walked out to the car where Duane Yancey was still barricaded.

"Roll that window down, boy!" ordered the marshal. "What's this I hear about you being after Mrs. Tate's body?"

While Yancey tried to explain, Mrs. Tate saw him and recognized him as her new roomer.

"I told him, no keeping late hours, marshal! I told him, if he was a Methodist, he could just smoke his cigars somewhere else!"

Yancey tried again to explain. Mrs. Tate told him he could stay there that night but he would have to move in the morning.

"I won't have a tap dancer or a snare drummer under my roof," she said.

12

Big Rafe Goes Home

Alta Munger, wife of Big Rafe and mother of the felon Rafe, Jr., sat in the den of the Munger home, a split-level ranch style with double carport, on Alta Drive, two blocks off Main Street. When Big Rafe had laid out the subdivision, he had named the street after her. He named the street behind it Rafe, Jr. Drive.

It was ten-thirty Friday evening, and Alta Munger was working the crossword puzzle that appeared daily in the Memphis *Commercial Appeal.* For a puzzle in a Memphis newspaper, it was very difficult, with words like "Italian River," two letters Down, and "Russian Coin," five letters Across. Alta Munger was not bright, but she finished it, in about an hour, every evening. She forced it. Sometimes she would put two letters in one square. It did not matter to her if it made sense, as long as every block had a letter in it.

Big Rafe drove up outside, entered the house by the side door in the carport, and stepped into the kitchen. He opened the refrigerator and took out a cold can of Diet Seven-Up, popped the top, and went into the den.

Big Rafe sat down. There was nothing said between them for a moment or two. Finally, "Rafe, Jr. is in trouble again."

"I know. I heard. What is it this time, exactly?"

"Drunk driving. We can count on that. Wrecking a car. Totalled out a sporty little Pimp. With factory air. Sula Measles, she's claiming he raped her. He tried to run Senator Oscar S. Baymule off the road. Rape, assault, drunk driving, attempted murder. He's going to be sent away this time. There's nothing I can do to save him. Money's going to mean nothing. Oscar S. Baymule is going to see him put away."

Alta continued to force the crossword puzzle.

"Parchman?" she asked.

"I'm afraid so."

More silence, then Alta spoke. "I'd almost rather he be in the pen than to be married to that Davy Sue Merkle, that snake chunker's daughter! I had my heart set on him marrying the Queen of Delta Gamma Gam!"

"I wish you'd see Davy Sue's good side!"

"That's just another bidness deal, you fixing up that marriage! Who'd ever believe you'd marry off your son to a bony, ninety-pound tomboy just because she can add up a column of figures!"

"Not only just add! Subtract! Divide! Multiply! That girl is a walking IBM calculator! She's a genius! And smart, too! I want her to be in charge of the books when I get the Roller Board Inn going. You've gotta have a bookkeeper! That's the first lesson you learn in bidness. Books's gotta be kept! Why, I'll have a dozen Roller Board Inns before it's over, maybe two dozen! There'll be books and more books to keep and Davy Sue will keep them and I'll trust her because she'll be family! She'll be my daughter-in-law!"

Alta threw down her crossword puzzle. "You and your deals! Your big plans have ruined my life! Rafe, I'm borne to death! I'm miserable! I wish it was like it was, back in the beginning! I want to go back to the days when all you had was eight or ten nigger rent houses!"

"A man's gotta keep on moving, Alta. I've told you that, time and again. Onward and onward. Richer and richer."

"Well, at least, there'll be no wedding as long as Rafe, Jr. is in jail."

Big Rafe shook his head. "You're wrong there. The wedding'll take place, as scheduled. By proxy. It's all been taken care of. There'll be a proxy for Rafe, Jr. I've already had it put in the paper. Rafe, Jr. got called up by the National Guard and a fraternity brother from Ole Miss is going to stand in for him."

"You did what?" asked Alta, in shock. "A proxy?"

"I had to. The Roller Board deal will fall through if it gets out up in Memphis about Rafe, Jr. You know how Roller Board won't give a franchise to anyone without good morals all the way down the line. We have to go through with the wedding! I've already invited the Executive Vice-President for High Rises for the whole Roller Board chain! If I had to call him and say, 'It's off,' he'd start looking into it and find out about Rafe, Jr., and there'd be no franchise. No franchise, and we'd be broke! I've got to get that franchise so I can get financing. Damn it, Alta, you know I've given the Stucco brothers a hot check for that option. We're hocked up to the neck! Doc Dennis is hocked! Tubby Turmath is hocked! I gotta work angles! I gotta make deals! I gotta get that franchise!"

"What a mess we're in!" said Alta.

"Mess is right," said Big Rafe. "But we've been in spots before! We made out all right!"

Alta looked out the picture window.

"Maybe we'll make out all right this time," she said.

"We will. We will."

"All the same," said Alta, "I'm not going to the wedding! I am not going to set foot in that Merkle house and make out like I'm happy about it!"

Big Rafe smote his forehead. "You've got to go! The Executive Vice-President will want to meet you! You know that! You've got to go!"

"I will NOT go!" said Alta, and she left the room.

Big Rafe sat there in the den, drinking Diet Seven-Up and trying to think of an angle.

He thought of one! The Executive Vice-President did not know what Alta Munger looked like. He would hire a woman to pose as his wife! Big Rafe smiled, for the first time that day.

"Rafe Munger!" he said aloud to himself. "When it comes to working angles, they ain't a suh mitch in northwest Mississippi to hold a candle to you!"

13

Saturday Morning in Bloat

An old pickup truck, battered and dented, with no state license plates, only a metal tag bought at Stuckey's that read, "GOD IS THE ANSWER," moved slowly down Main Street, from the water tower toward the road out to the Barrow Pits. Ricey Fitts was at the wheel, holding it with his left hand. In his right hand was a duck caller, the kind for sale in a Sears sporting goods department. Whenever he saw a Negro woman on the street, he slowed down as he went past her, put the duck caller to his lips and quacked obscenely.

Ricey Fitts was the only man from Bloat, Mississippi ever to hold a state office in the Veterans of Foreign Wars.

He drove up and down Main Street three times, then pulled up and angle-parked in front of the Spit Cafe. It was about eight o'clock in the morning and the Spit was filling up with regulars. Ricey Fitts sat at a table with three old friends: one, a man who drove the "bottle" gas truck; one, a salesman for Dixie Midget Corn Meal; and the third, a foreman at the axe-handle factory before he retired.

Ricey ordered coffee and started looking around.

A stranger sat at the table next to him, a heavy, fleshy man about thirty, with curly blonde hair. At first glance, he looked fat, but on second glance, just big. It was Jackie Bad Ass, a professional wrestler out of Memphis, who had been in Jackson, Mississippi, the night before, wrestling for the Southern Heavyweight Championship.

Jackie Bad Ass had a big tattoo, Jesus choking an eagle, on his upper right arm and he was wearing leather sandals with lots of brass rings and studs on them. He was finishing breakfast, four eggs, fried over light, and was sopping up the yellow with buttered toast.

Ricey Fitts noticed the stranger's sandals.

"That's something I ain't never seen before," he said to his friends. "Sandals on a man."

The three friends turned to look at Jackie Bad Ass's sandals.

"Sandals on a man. That mean's just one thing," said Ricey Fitts. "There sits a fruit!"

"Our Lord and Savior wore sandals!" said the corn meal salesman. "I seen pitchurs in the Bobble!"

"Sandals on a man," repeated Ricey Fitts. "There sits a fruit!"

Jackie Bad Ass heard him say it. He set a piece of toast dripping with egg yolk back on his plate, wiped his lips with a paper napkin, and turned around and faced Ricey Fitts.

"Did I hear you say that I might be wearing a fruit's shoe?" he asked.

Ricey Fitts got flustered. "No sir! All I said was, that's one thing I never have seen before, sandals on a man!"

"How'd you like to have one of them up between the cheeks of your ass?" asked the wrestler.

Ricey Fitts turned away from Jackie Bad Ass and said, under his breath, to his friends, "He may be a fruit but he talks just like you and I do!"

Jackie Bad Ass finished breakfast and picked up his check and walked up front to Mom, at the cashier's counter.

"You got any bul gum?" he asked.

"The only gum we got, honey, is ABC gum!"

"What kind is that?" asked Jackie Bad Ass.

"Already been choon!" said Mom, and she broke out in a cackle.

Jackie Bad Ass laughed, too, then bought some sugarless gum that cleaned the teeth while it sweetened the breath.

Mom walked over to the table where Ricey Fitts and his friends were sitting. "Who is that boy?" she asked. "The way he talks, he must be from around here someplace, but I never seen him before."

"You mean that fruit?" asked Ricey Fitts.

''Did I hear you say I might be wearing a fruit's shoe?''

"What do you mean, 'fruit'?" asked Mom.
"Sandals on a man," said Ricey Fitts.
"Sandals on a man don't mean a fruit!" said Mom. "It's when a man carries uh numbrella that he's a fruit!"

Big Rafe had walked over to the Mink Motel to pick up Rixie Leaptrot and Bunny and take them to the Spit Cafe for breakfast. He stopped at the desk.
"What room's Mr. Leaptrot in?" he asked.
"I moan' a kill you!" said the clerk.
Big Rafe adjusted his glasses and took another look at the clerk.
"Oh, it that you, Coy?" he asked. "Still not feeling any better?"
Coy's father, Coy Mink, Sr., appeared and said, "Your friend's in number 12. Sorry, Mr. Munger, about Coy. He's taking treatments."
"I understand," said Big Rafe.
Coy Mink, Sr. leaned across the desk and whispered in Big Rafe's ear, "Sometimes I worry, with him having keys to the rooms and all."
Big Rafe found his new friends awake. Rixie Leaptrot was in the bathroom, shaving his ear lobes.
The three of them walked out past the desk. Rixie Leaptrot cut his eyes in the direction of Coy Mink, Jr., who sat behind the desk, honing a Bowie knife on an Arkansas stone.
"That boy's not all there!" he said. "Dangerous, I say!"
"He's taking treatments," said Big Rafe.

They walked to the Spit Cafe and got there just as Ricey Fitts was coming out the door.
He grabbed Big Rafe by the shirt sleeve.
"I hear they're holding Rafe, Jr.! I hear they got him on drunk driving! I hear he totalled out a brand new Pimp! I hear when the marshal pulled him out of the wreck, he was stoon to the gills!"
Ricey Fitts did not wait for an answer. He got in his pickup truck and drove off down Main, his duck caller going to beat sixty.
"That's Ricey Fitts," said Big Rafe to Rixie Leaptrot and Bunny. "His granddaddy used to have Ricey Fitts Lumber Company. Worth a couple million dollars in the Twenties, until Ricey's daddy lost it all trying to make plywood. Ricey, he don't do a thing these days, except quack dirty duck calls at nigger women."
Over breakfast — hot cakes, waffles with blueberry syrup and dairy butter, King Cotton Baby Link sausages, orange juice and

coffee — Big Rafe laid out plans for the coming week.

"I put it out that Rafe, Jr. got called up overnight by the National Guard. I told them Bunny here was a frat brother at Ole Miss and a two-time winner of Mr. Popularity and that he was going to stand up for Rafe, Jr. at the wedding."

Bunny had a second helping of everything.

"That boy," asked Big Rafe, in a whisper. "Can't he talk?"

"Bunny's a mute, that's what he is," said Rixie Leaptrot. "He can hear like a bell but he can't say a word."

"Ain't that awful!" said Big Rafe. "Awful! A good-looking fella like him. MORE COFFEE, BUNNY?"

"I'll have a cup, Big Rafe," said a woman who walked up to the table and sat down, uninvited. It was Wolfena Poppenbarger, Society Editor of the *Titus County Tomcat.* She was about fifty, had prominent teeth and wore green eye shadow and lots of gold bracelets with bangles and charms on them. Miss Poppenbarger smoked a cigarette in a short holder and wore sequined eyeglasses that made her look like The Cat Woman.

If she had stepped out on the streets of Bloat in her bangles and green eye shadow in the old days, twenty years ago, she would have been brought up before the Justice of the Peace, old man Fritz Pitts, and fined ten dollars for appearing in the trappings of a harlot. Judge Pitts once fined a famous colored band leader ten dollars for driving through Bloat, Mississippi while barefooted and it made Walter Winchell. For the last two years of his life, Judge Pitts had cancer of the mouth and had to be fed with an air hose.

"What's happened to Rafe, Jr.?" asked Wolfena Poppenbarger, after she sat down. "Is he in some kind of trouble? I hear he's in trouble again. It's nothing to do with that sporty little Pimp that's been pulled into Blackie's Body Shop, is it? I hear it's totalled out and that Rafe, Jr. was seen driving it yesterday afternoon."

"Rafe, Jr. is not in any trouble, Wolfena," said Big Rafe, smiling paternally. "He's been called up by the National Guard. Secret Mission. Don't know when he'll be back."

"What about the wedding? I read in the *Tomcat* this morning that it was going ahead, with a proxy to stand up for Rafe, Jr. How can that be?"

"This here's the proxy," said Big Rafe, pointing to Bunny. "Mr. ... er ..."

"Whitesides," said Rixie Leaptrot. He stood up and extended his hand to Wolfena Poppenbarger. "I'm Rixie Leaptrot and this here is Bunny Whitesides. My folks was circus people."

"Bunny was a frat brother of Rafe, Jr.'s at Ole Miss," said Big Rafe, "and a two-time winner of Mr. Popularity."

Wolfena Poppenbarger extended her hand to Bunny.

It was Wolfena's first proxy wedding.

"Bunny's got a bad throat this morning and can't talk," said Big Rafe.

"You say Rafe, Jr. is not in any trouble?" she asked.

"Not a bit," said Big Rafe. "Just off serving his country."

"Maybe so," she said. "Maybe so. All I know is, the Methodist Church Young People were not allowed to roller skate on the jail floor last night, and it the night they were supposed to crown the Queen!"

"You got me!" said Big Rafe, throwing up his hands.

Wolfena Poppenbarger hurried out of the Spit, to the *Tomcat* office, to check it all out.

"Where's the wedding to be?" asked Rixie Leaptrot, after she had left.

"The bride's house," said Big Rafe. "That's the way she wanted it. Get married at home, that's her idea. The house is too small. I tried to get her to have it at the Bloat Country Club, or at least, the American Legion Hut, but she said 'No.' That girl's just got to have her way! Ornery as they make 'em. Wanted to get married at home so she could parade down a stairs, or something. You know how a woman can be! Stubborn! But that girl! Smart! Why, she can add up a double column of figures in her head quicker than a canebreak patcher eatin' grillits!"

"The bride's people — " asked Rixie Leaptrot. "They have money?"

"Not a penny! White trash! White trash, that's what they are! They rent a house from me. I have to threaten to read them out every month! Her mother used to wait table here in the Spit and her daddy is nothing but a snake-chunking preacher. A nut! That's what he is, a nut! He's running for the school board, right now, on a platform of 'Every Man His Own Bible Prophet!'"

"That's a nut, to me!" said Rixie Leaptrot.

Big Rafe took a notebook out of his pocket.

"There's three or four things you've got to do before the wedding," he said. "First, you and Bunny will have to go up to Memphis and rent tuxedos. Davy Sue has got some nonsense color thing going. Everybody's got to wear lime green tuxedos. Me, the groom, the best man, the ushers. Her cousin, Buddy, who's going to sing, him, everybody. There's a place up in Memphis that rents loud tuxedos for nigger high school dances. You can get them there. Davy Sue'll go with you. She knows where it is.

"Second, there's a stag party being given for Rafe, Jr. by Toddy Alexander, next Thursday night, out at Rosecliff Plantation. Toddy's just about the richest young man in this part of the state. Him and his two brothers inherited Rosecliff Plantation. All three of them been all the way through Ole Miss, still there's not a one of them can even write his own name.

"I'd cancel out on the party, I'd make some excuse for Rafe, Jr., if I could think of any way, but I can't. You two will have to go, whether you want to or not. It'll be a big party — three, four hundred guests. Lots of barbecue, beer. Rixie, you take Bunny along and just say he's got a bad throat. You'd better not mention that Mr. Popularity thing there, though. Everybody at the party will have been to Ole Miss and they'll know Bunny never went."

"We could say he was Mr. Popularity at the University of Arkansas," said Rixie. "That's far enough away, nobody will know any better."

"That might work," said Big Rafe.

Bunny was finishing up a piece of Boston Creme Pie, made by the Supreme Pie Company of Memphis and delivered fresh every Tuesday.

Big Rafe, Rixie Leaptrot and Bunny Whitesides walked out of the Spit as Duane Yancey, the new reporter for the *Titus County Tomcat,* walked in. Yancey had come for his first breakfast in the town he planned to take by storm. He sat down at the counter and picked up a menu.

The three men who had been sitting with Ricey Fitts saw Yancey enter and nodded to each other. They had been waiting for him.

"That's him!" said one.

"That's the suh mitch!"

"That's him all right!"

The three men walked over to the counter and sat down by Yancey, two on one side, one on the other.

"Finish up your breakfast," said one. "Then get out of town!"

"What?" asked Yancey. "What did you say? What is this?"

"We don't need your kind in Bloat, Mississippi," said one of the men.

"What are you guys talking about?"

"The marshal said he couldn't prove nothing, but it looked to him last night like you was trying to rape Mrs. Tate."

"We don't need rapers here!" said one of the men.

All this talk was in whispers, under the breath, *sotto voce,* and nobody else in the Spit knew what was going on.

"Finish up your breakfast, then get out of town," repeated one of the men.

"We don't need your kind in Bloat, Mississippi," repeated another.

Duane Yancey looked at the faces of the three men. Tiny red eyes, close together. Little rat teeth. They had little hands with short, pointed fingers. There was not much of a gene pool in Bloat,

Mississippi. The men had their hair cut close and their necks were red.

Yancey decided they meant business.

"We mean bidness," said one of the men.

"OK," said Yancey. "I got you. I'll get out."

"That's smart," said one.

"I'll have to pack. It'll be an hour or two before I can get things together."

"One hour. Two hours. That's fine. Just don't let us catch you in town when the Spit puts out its dinner menu."

Duane Yancey got up and left the Spit. The three men remained at the counter. Mom came up with a glass of water and a waxed paper sleeve containing knife, fork and folded paper napkin.

"Where'd that boy go?" she asked.

"He remembered something."

"Had to leave."

"Won't be back."

Duane Yancey walked down Main Street to his car.

"Ku Kluxers!" he thought to himself. "I've just had a run-in with Ku Kluxers!"

He went out to Mrs. Tate's house and entered more easily than he had the night before. The dog was not there. He was at the vet's, having the window screen sawed off his hips.

Yancey packed everything in ten minutes and left Mrs. Tate's. He drove to the *Tomcat* office and stayed there just long enough to write out a long story about Rafe, Jr. — a story that contained everything the marshal had told him. Everything — the totalled-out Pimp, the rape charges, the dope hidden under the back seat, the link with the big city vice rings,the possibility that Rafe, Jr. was responsible for two recent unsolved murders in the next county and the certainty that Rafe, Jr., son of prominent Bloat businessman Rafe Munger Land Deals, would be sent to Parchman Farm — then he called it in to the Associated Press and the *Commercial Appeal* in Memphis.

In an hour, Duane Yancey was headed north on the highway back to Memphis, where he planned to land another newspaper job on the strength of that story.

Davy Sue and her brother Frank attended Sunday school when they were children.

14

Bloat Goes to Church on Sunday Morning

Frank Merkle, Davy Sue's brother, City Editor of the *Titus County Tomcat* and ambulance driver for Mutt Brothers Funeral Home, and his wife, Juney Garland Merkle (named for the movie star by her ignorant parents), occupied a one-room apartment in her parents' house. Their radio was tuned to a twenty-four-hour Country Gospel station in Memphis and turned down low.

Her parents were Church of Christ and did not like noise. Music made them itch, and they had threatened to go up on the rent if they ever heard any of it.

Merkle and his wife were dressing up to go to church. Juney Garland was getting into a purple dress with a flowered belt. She though it was too long and would much rather have worn her lavender pantsuit, but they did not let women in pantsuits enter her church.

"I'm going to have to have something new to wear before next Saturday," said Juney Garland. "Something I can wear to the wedding."

"All you ever want to do is spin money!"

"If you'd ever bring any home, it wouldn't make any difference how much I spin!"

"Quit riding me about how much I make! You know there ain't no money to be made in this town."

"If Davy Sue's gonna be so rich after Saturday, it's going to be embarrassing to me to live here, with no more money than you bring home!" said Juney Garland.

"What are you talking about?"

"We better move to Memphis!"

"Move to Memphis? I thought you didn't want to leave your people."

"Them fools?"

"That's what I always thought. That's what I told the new boy at the *Tomcat,* just the other day."

"Well, you got it wrong. I want to move to Memphis!"

"Well, I don't!"

"Why can't we move to Memphis like everybody else does, and you get on at Kellogg or Delta Battery?"

"I've told you one hundred times! I mean to write! You wait until there's a big murder down here and see if I don't write it up for *True Detective!*"

"And there's another thing! I want to have a little ole baby!"

"I don't want no kids!"

"I want to have a little ole baby and name him Dewey Dave. Dewey Dave Merkle!"

"Forget that! I've tole you!"

"Brother Pond ast me a day or two ago why we hadn't yet had a little ole baby. He said the Lord meant for people to have little ole babies!"

"Brother Pond? That kid? What the Hell's that kid talking to you about things like babies for? I oughta bust his ass!"

"Don't you talk like that about Brother Pond! He may be just fifteen years old, but he's an ordained Baptist preacher!

"Ordained or not, I don't like him!"

"If you talk bad about him, the Lord'll strike you down!"

"It ain't natural, a fifteen-year-old kid being a preacher!"

"Like him or not, he's performing your sister's wedding. She likes him! She thinks he's got the Call!"

They had finished dressing up to go to church. Frank was in his double-knit shirt with black and white check, his striped necktie and his double-knit herringbone suit with the belt in the back. Juney Garland had on the purple dress and a pair of white plastic sandals.

Off to church.

"Really, now, why don't we move to Memphis? You could get a job. I see in the paper all the time, they want manager trainees for those Taco Bell places. We could get us an apartment in Memphis, one of those out by the Expressway."

"What would we do for furniture?" asked Frank, sullenly.

"You can get fifteen pieces of furniture for $149.00 at Railroad Salvage."

"Me, manage a Taco Bell! Damn, but you sure don't understand me!"

"Do you just hafta cuss on Sunday?"

Frank and Juney Garland sat in a pew next to his mother and his sister, Davy Sue, at the New Bethel Baptist Church. His father had not come. Old man Merkle never went to church. He conducted his worship services in his garage, where he kept his snakes. Daddy Merkle would not enter a Baptist Church. Too formal. "You might as well go Catholic on me, as to go to a formal church," he always said.

Brother Pond was in the pulpit. He wore glasses and had a high voice. Whenever he talked to a stranger on the telephone, he always had to explain he was a boy, not a girl. Brother Pond was not the actual preacher at New Bethel. Brother Buell Mealer was the actual preacher but Brother Pond preached every third Sunday. He had been ordained when he was thirteen years old and had already conducted two funerals and a baptism.

Brother Pond was well into his sermon.

"... I know they's young people out there ... puffin' on cigarettes. Drinkin' wine. Drinkin' beer. Drinkin' whiskey. Ridin' motorcycles. Makin' mock ... "

He finished his sermon and the choir finished singing the last hymn. It was time for the Invitational, that moment when one wanting to be Saved could come forward to the pulpit and make his decision for Christ.

A little girl, six or seven, with crossed eyes, got up from her seat and walked toward Brother Pond. When she reached the pulpit he took her hand and asked, "Do you accept the Lord Jesus Christ as your Personal Savior?"

"I guess so," said the little girl.

Brother Pond was elated. It was the first time his preaching had moved someone in the congregation to come forward and be Saved.

Davy Sue and her mother shook hands with Brother Pond as they left the church.

"I guess you heard about Rafe, Jr., having to have a proxy for the wedding next Saturday, Brother Pond," said Davy Sue.

"No, I hadn't. A proxy? What's that?"

"It's a substitute. Rafe, Jr. got called up by the National Guard and a frat brother from Ole Miss is going to stand up for him."

Davy Sue felt bad about lying to the preacher, even if he was just a kid.

Brother Pond was troubled. After the congregation had left, he went downstairs to the office of Brother Buell Mealer. Brother Mealer was clearing up things, stacking song books, putting away Bibles, wrapping pennies, getting ready to leave, and saying aloud, "What Joy Today!" in a hearty voice, to no one in particular.

"I've got to talk to you, Brother Mealer," said Brother Pond. "I'm troubled."

"What about, Brother Pond?"

"The wedding next Saturday."

"Nothing to worry about. A young preacher is always nervous when he performs his first wedding. Nothing to it. You'll do fine!"

"It's not that part of it I'm worried about. What I'm worried about is what the Lord will think, my performing a wedding with Rafe, Jr., as the groom. He's not Saved. He's not even thinking about being Saved! Won't it be mocking the Lord if I perform the wedding?"

Brother Mealer was in a hurry to get home to Sunday dinner. He was having fried squirrel. His brother-in-law had brought in a mess, even though it was out of season. If there was one thing Brother Mealer loved, it was a fried summer squirrel.

"I see what you mean, Brother Pond. Rafe, Jr., is no-account, that's right enough. But I believe the Lord will straighten him out, after the wedding."

Neither clergyman knew that Rafe, Jr., was confined in the jail at that moment, awaiting disposition of some serious charges against him.

"But I cannot unite in marriage a good woman like Davy Sue with a bad man like Rafe, Jr. He drinks. He mocks. He's dispectful to his elders!"

Brother Mealer always felt uncomfortable around Brother Pond. It was eerie, creepy, being around a fifteen-year-old boy who always wore a navy blue suit and a black tie.

"I think everything will work out all right," said Brother Mealer.

"I think it's wrong to marry them. It's against what I've been taught to believe."

"The Lord will work everything out after the wedding."

"But Rafe, Jr., has even been seen riding a motorcycle!"

"The Lord will take care of it. After the wedding."

"My mind's going around in a circle. I haven't been able to

sleep at night."

"You need to get out more! Have fun! A young fella like you! Why don't you go along on the Young People's hayride next Saturday night?"

"They're filthy, hayrides! Nothing but Temptation! Temptation on wheels!"

Brother Mealer put on his coat and started toward the door. "What Joy Today!" he boomed to the world, then left the building.

Brother Pond's own parents always addressed him as "Brother Pond."

"Will Brother Pond give the Blessing?" asked his mother, after the Pond family had sat down for Sunday dinner.

They were having baked capon and sweet potatoes. Brother Pond ate little. He was jittery, and sweat was pouring off him. Long before the others had finished, he left the table and went upstairs to his room.

He loosened his necktie and sat in a chair, looking at the wall. The problem of Rafe, Jr. was foremost in his mind. He was worried to death. If he united Davy Sue Merkle with Rafe, Jr., the Lord would strike him blind, the same as He would if He caught him playing with himself. Thank the Lord, that was one thing Brother Pond did not have to worry about. He had not played with himself since he was Saved, two years ago.

Late in the afternoon, Brother Pond made his decision. He would not perform the ceremony as long as Rafe, Jr. was not Saved. If the Lord reached out to Rafe, Jr. and touched him, and made him see the light, and Rafe, Jr. accepted the Lord Jesus Christ as his Savior, THEN he would perform the ceremony. Until then, there would be no wedding, no matter who suffered, no matter what plans were upset.

Rafe, Jr. was the Devil's own, and that was all there was to it. That much was clear to Brother Pond, but he was still disturbed by Brother Mealer's attitude. Brother Mealer was all for going ahead with the wedding and then letting the Lord work his miracles. That was wrong! Brother Pond knew it was wrong! Brother Mealer would have married anyone, even the Devil himself, to Davy Sue. Brother Pond had lost his respect for Brother Mealer. Mealer was a man who would take the easy way out.

Brother Pond sat in his room all afternoon, quietly, looking at the wall and trying to understand the ways of the Lord and Brother Mealer and trying to find some way to tell his parents and Brother Mealer and Davy Sue that he would not perform the wedding under the present conditions.

15

Monday: Coy Mink, Jr. Goes to Memphis for His "Treatment"

Coy Mink and his wife sat at their breakfast table, sipping coffee and looking out the window at their sweet peas.

"It's time to wake up Coy, Jr.," said Mrs. Mink. "You know how long it takes him to get ready."

"You're right," said Coy Mink. "We wouldn't want him to be late."

"Coy, do you think those treatments are doing him any good?"

"Don't seem to be."

Coy Mink, Jr. was "taking treatments." Every Monday morning, his father drove him to Memphis for a session with his psychiatrist at the Gailor Clinic of the University of Tennessee Center for the Health Sciences.

"At a hundred dollars a visit, I think that psychiatrist ought to be doing him more good," said Mrs. Mink.

"Looks to me like they ought to be giving him some pills, some kind of tranquilizers, or something."

"Maybe the psychiatrist knows what he's doing."

"Coy, Jr. says he's some kind of foreigner."

"That's encouraging," said Mrs. Mink. "Foreigners have more sense than we do."

"Sigmund Freud was a foreigner!"

"That's what I'm talking about! They say Coy, Jr.'s psychiatrist is the very best in Memphis!"

"Nothing's too good for our boy!" said Coy Mink. "I'll go wake him up."

"And I'll get his breakfast ready!"

Coy Mink tiptoed into the bedroom of Coy Mink, Jr. Nothing in the room was out of place. That was one thing you could say for Coy Mink, Jr. He was neat as a pin.

The old man touched his son's shoulder and shook him gently. "Coy! Coy, son! Time to get up! Time to go to Memphis!"

"Suck uh aig, ole man!" said Coy, Jr., from within the bedding.

"Time to wake up, Coy!"

"I'm not asleep. I been awake all night."

Coy Mink, Jr. got out of bed, showered, dressed in his black suit, white shirt, black tie and black shoes and entered the breakfast room. Mrs. Mink had set out his orange juice, All-Bran and a small portion of hot mashed potatoes. She believed that a serving of mashed potatoes every morning at breakfast would keep the bowels open.

Coy, Jr. sat down at the table, drank the orange juice, then toyed with the cereal.

"Sit up straight!" said Mrs. Mink.

"Sit up straight, Coy," said Mr. Mink. "You wouldn't want your back to grow crooked, would you?"

Coy, Jr. straightened up and ate the cereal, then started to leave the table.

"Eat your potatoes!" said Mrs. Mink.

"I don't like arsh potatoes," said Coy, Jr.

"Eat them!" said Mrs. Mink. "They're good for you!"

"Eat them, Coy," said Mr. Mink. "You don't want to get sick, do you?"

Coy, Jr. ate the potatoes, then he and his father got in the car and headed north to Memphis. Mr. Mink drove. Coy, Jr. was supposed to be there at eight o'clock.

Patients are always supposed to be there at eight o'clock. The doctors come in at eleven-thirty. Mr. Mink drove sixty-five all the way and they got to the door of the Gailor Clinic at ten minutes until eight o'clock.

Coy, Jr. got out of the car and waved goodbye as it pulled away. Eight o'clock in the morning. His father would be back for him at four-thirty. It aways took from eight o'clock until four-thirty to have a session with the psychiatrist.

Coy Mink, Jr. was taking treatments.

Coy Mink, Jr. entered the Gailor Clinic building and passed through halls filled with old, sick, poor black people in wheelchairs or on stretchers, vomiting, bleeding, dying, past long lines of poor people waiting for X-rays or blood tests or prescriptions.

The crippled black midget who sold snacks to the waiting patients had his wares — Mrs. Drake's tuna sandwiches on raisin bread, oranges, candy bars, potato chips and Dolly Madison pastries — spread across a bench between a spastic old man and a black woman about to deliver.

Coy Mink, Jr. took the elevator to the sixth floor, to the Psychiatry waiting room.

"I'm Coy Mink, Jr., here for my appointment," he said to the receptionist.

"Have a seat, Mr. Mink. Dr. Baggazippian will be with you as soon as possible."

Coy Mink, Jr. sat down in one of the chairs. He knew it would be a long wait. It always was.

There were others in the waiting room. Among them, the usual five or six very fat women who hoped to lose weight through pyschiatry; a female dwarf who had no love life, her little legs dangling from her chair; a dashing young woman in a flowing cape, cowboy boots, skin-tight pants and a beige suede-leather hat with a floppy brim decorated with the entire plumage of one South Dakota pheasant. She was a mime who had once studied with Vendetta La Blanc.

A young man with a beard and the eyes of a dope fiend sat twitching across the room from Coy Mink, Jr. He wanted badly to smoke a marijuana cigarette or, failing that, to shoot something, anything — ground roach powder, fennel, wheat paste — into his veins, or so he kept telling the receptionist.

Two matrons, who looked like they might be preachers' wives — well, higher than that, ministers' wives — sat quietly, tears occasionally escaping their eyes.

The gathering sat silently for a long time, an hour, maybe more, without anyone saying anything. Everyone was waiting to see his doctor.

The bearded hippie suddenly went wild.

He jumped up, grabbed a copy of *Field and Stream* and opened it to a page and pointed his finger at it.

"You don't ever have to *read* a magazine," he said, excitedly. "All you have to do is look at the pictures! That's all *I* ever do!"

He circled the room, repeating the statement to everyone, individually.

"I wish there were some *real* kids here," he said. "They'd understand!"

Then he got down on his knees and started crawling along the floor. Everyone looked at him but no one stirred. No one, that is, but the receptionist. She called the security office and soon two old men, both palsied to the point of disability, dressed in uniforms and carrying lots of guns, blackjacks, keys and flashlights, arrived in the waiting room and took the hippie in charge.

The older of the guards saluted the receptionist as they took the hippie out, and said, "You need us, little lady, you call us!"

"'Preciate it, Mr. Peach!" said the receptionist.

The waiting room settled back down again.

"What will they do with him?" asked the dashing young woman in the plumage of one South Dakota pheasant.

"What?" asked the receptionist.

"What will they do with him?"

"Oh, I don't know. Chemotherapy, I guess."

"I'll tell you what they'll do with him!" said a man in the waiting room. "They'll take him downstairs and stick needles in his ass until they break him! That's what they'll do!"

It seemed to the dashing young lady that everyone in the waiting room was looking at her. Sweat broke out on her forehead. It was probably the cape she was wearing. Anyone ought to know better than to wear a cape in Memphis in the summertime. Even a nut!

"I'm into street mime," she said, nervously, to the room.

"What's street mime?" asked one of the fat women.

"I act, in the streets! Mime! I become birds, children, flowers opening to the sun!"

"Why?" asked the fat woman.

"Because it's beautiful!"

"Do you make anything out of it?"

"I don't do it to make money!"

"How do you live?"

"I make people happy! They give me food and a bed for the night!"

"That seems dangerous to me," said the fat woman.

"I'll give you a bed for the night," said the man who knew what they were going to do to the hippie. "I'll give you a bed, any night." He was a war veteran who believed he had been poisoned by the air in Korea in 1953.

The receptionist interrupted the discussion by saying: "Miss Tapsie Bobo? You can go in now."

The female dwarf had been dozing in her chair. At the mention of her name, she came to, with a jerk. She took a lipstick, Countess Carla's Pink Sleet, from her purse and applied it to her upper lip, then rubbed her lips together until they were both covered. Miss Bobo jumped down from her chair and walked like a duck toward the door to the doctor's office.

A twitter of laughter ran through the waiting room and she turned angrily toward the other patients and said:

"I din ast to be barn!"

The receptionist opened the door to the doctor's office for her.

Again, there was silence.

One of the ministers' wives, seeing Coy Mink, Jr. in his black suit, white shirt, black tie and black shoes, took him for a ministerial student, perhaps one who could not accept sex or the Scriptures, and spoke softly to him.

"Are you in the seminary?"

Coy Mink, Jr. shook his head. "I'm desk clerk at a motel. Mink Motel. Bloat, Mississippi. Downtown Bloat. It's my daddy's."

"What's troubling you, son?" asked the minister's wife.

"I want to kill everyone on earth. I even want to kill my own mommy and daddy. Especially them."

The minister's wife was shocked. She recoiled, then checked her purse to be sure the tear gas gun was in it. If he jumped her, she would splat him right in the face with it. It would not kill him. Just make him harmless. Harmless, until the security officers with their blackjacks could get there and slap the stew out of him.

The receptionist said, "Mr. Mink, you can go in now."

It was nearly eleven-thirty in the morning. Coy Mink, Jr. had been sitting in the waiting room over three hours. He entered the door behind the receptionist.

He was met by a psychiatric social worker, a young man in stacked heels and tight pants, carrying a green canvas purse on a strap over his shoulder. The social worker laughed a lot. He was taking something to elevate his mood. Working around all those mental cases had made him depressed and when even his own cats began to notice it, he asked one of the staff psychiatrists to give him something to cheer him up. He took too much of it and now laughed too much, sometimes inappropriately.

"Ready for the relaxing room, Mr. Mink?" he asked. "How are you feeling today?"

"I want to kill everyone on earth, starting with you."

The social worker laughed until his sides nearly split. Then he escorted Coy Mink, Jr. into the relaxing room and helped him into the electric Relax-a-Chair and adjusted the headrest. He tightened the safety straps down across Coy Mink, Jr.'s chest and legs, then turned down the lights and started the machinery.

The chair began to undulate softly. Soothing movements, a gentle flow, as on a calm lake. A silver screen descended into place on the wall opposite the Relax-a-Chair and a motion picture projector began to show restful scenes upon it: mountains in Switzerland; beaches in Tahiti; fields of yellow flowers, blowing in the wind; puppies at play; children, beautiful children, right out of cereal or clothing advertisements, stringing brightly colored glass beads and laughing.

The social worker tiptoed out of the room.

While the restful scenes were playing on the wall, the voice of a well-bred woman came into the room through a concealed speaker, a calming voice, warm, melodious, reading from the poetry of Kenrod Dreary.

My home hall smells of cinnamon brill,
and roses glane and bay birch thrill.

And softly shadows climb the hill...

Coy Mink, Jr. was strapped tightly into the Relax-a-Chair. Patients are left in the chair for about twenty minutes to be soothed before seeing the psychiatrist, the current theory being that the session in the chair made them more receptive to therapy.

Dr. Baggazippian should have arrived in the building about the time Coy Mink, Jr. was placed in the chair and he should have seen him in his office soon after. Today, however he was late. He was lunching at the faculty club, on fifteen chicken livers wrapped in bacon and baked tomatoes stuffed with bread crumbs and Parmesan cheese, when a colleague, a Dr. Shalto Sprague, from Gipsy Hill, London, England, stopped at his table and said:

"At home, you know, they are called chicken's liv-ah! I believe you chaps call it chicken liv-ahs! Do you not?"

Dr. Baggazippian did not understand English very well and his foreign accent made *him* difficult to understand. He tried to reply to the comment of Dr. Sprague.

"Glossona reech no humma!" he said.

"Chicken's LIV-AH!" repeated Dr. Sprague.

Dr. Baggazippian thought he was being insulted and he leapt for the other man's throat, such being the custom among his people.

Some of the other diners separated the two men.

Dr. Sprague left the dining room muttering, "That fellow's balmy! Crackers, he is! Daft as a lord!"

Dr. Baggazippian left the dining room and went into the faculty lounge, where he sat in a corner staring at the wall and contemplating legal action against Dr. Sprague. He quickly decided against going into the courts. If he did, it would surely come out that he was in the country illegally. Here, he was making a hundred dollars an hour. If they sent him home, he would have to go back to tending goats for a living. That would not be smart.

Coy Mink, Jr. was still strapped in the Relax-a-Chair, still undulating. He began to have hunger fantasies: A large sugar-cured ham, with pineapple slices and cherries; baked sweet potatoes, running with dairy butter; pies, cakes, apples and oranges, all floating in a giant vat of hot vegetable soup! He could almost taste the celery. The attendants forgot about him floating in the Relax-a-Chair until Dr. Baggazippian came in, three hours later.

No one knew anything about Dr. Baggazippian. His national origins were uncertain. He spoke a language no one had ever heard. His credentials, his *vita,* were written in symbols that no one, none of the other psychiatrists, not even the Arabs, Cubans or Balinese, who made up the department, had ever seen. He was thought to have published several articles in learned journals in the Arab states, which led some of his colleagues to believe he was an Arab.

Others thought he was from SouthAmerica.There were things about him that made him look like a South American. He wore a lot of silver jewelry and alligator or sea-turtle shoes and loud, wide neckties and pink suits and lots of foreign-smelling scents.

The chairman of the department, Dr. Willbanger, had thought he was a Gypsy when he hired him and assumed that he was a credit to his race.

Dr. Baggazippian entered his office and waited behind his desk while the social worker unstrapped Coy Mink, Jr. and freed him from the Relax-a-Chair. Coy Mink, Jr. staggered when he walked into Dr. Baggazippian's office. Dr. Baggazippian thought he must have been drinking and made an entry to that effect on Coy Mink, Jr.'s chart. Coy Mink, Jr. fell into the deep chair in front of the doctor's desk.

"Garn arftoon, glenn harna!" said the doctor.

Coy Mink, Jr. began his recital.

"I want to kill everybody on earth. Beginning with my own mommy and daddy."

Dr. Baggazippian made more notations on Coy Mink, Jr.'s chart.

"They're too nosy!" said Coy Mink, Jr. "They think they ought to know everything I keep in my room. I'll bet if I stuck a knife in each one of them, they'd keep their noses out of my room!"

"Splessa treena bosu boose!" said Dr. Baggazippian, somewhat tartly.

"I choked a puppy last week," said Coy Mink, Jr.

Dr. Baggazzipian wrote it down.

"Full blood St. Bernard. I put him in the cedar chest, right next to the winter blankets." Coy Mink, Jr. laughed. "They'll find it!" he said, and laughed some more.

Dr. Baggazippian wrote very rapidly on Coy Mink, Jr.'s chart, in his language of strange symbols.

"Garng sith?" he asked.

"The happiest day of my life will be the day when I get them both, Mommy and Daddy, right between the eyes."

Dr. Baggazippian nodded wisely. He shot his cuffs and admired his silver and turquoise links, then he looked Coy Mink, Jr. right in the eye and said, "Trista reeng TV?"

"Last night, I slipped into their bedroom. They were sound asleep. I could have got rid of them then."

Coy Mink, Jr., struck his fist into the palm of his other hand, in disgust with himself.

"Skeena reeng," said Dr. Baggazippian, shaking his head sadly. "Pozzy snumma. Pozzy, pozzy snumma!"

"I'll never have a chance like that again," said Coy Mink, Jr.

"Kunna Sands freena cheeks?"

In the next office, the social worker who laughed too much was interviewing a woman who had come to the Psychiatric Clinic for the first time. She was in her late twenties and already had five children and had come to the clinic because she was depressed and afraid and had been told they could help her. The social worker was asking her questions from a standard list.

Her answers were supposed to indicate her grasp of reality.

"If you were lost in the forest, how would you get out?" asked the social worker.

The women thought for a moment, twisting the strap on her handbag. Then her face brightened. "I'd follow the sun!" she said.

The social worker thought that was the funniest thing he had ever heard and laughed until he fell out of his chair.

Dr. Baggazippian heard the laughter through the walls of his office and glared in its direction.

"Sniss droppa soss!" he hissed. "Cot mitcha!"

Coy Mink, Jr. was continuing his recital.

"I want to get rid of Mommy and Daddy, then go on and get rid of everybody else. That's my life's goal. To get rid of everybody on earth."

Dr. Baggazippian looked at his watch. It had strange symbols on it. He may have been an Arab, but there were no Arabic numerals on his watch. It was time for Coy Mink's session to end. Dr. Baggazippian reached into his desk drawer and brought out a large container of capsules and handed it to Coy Mink, Jr. The doctor compounded his own medicines. The instructions for taking them were written on the container, in the same unidentified language that seemed to be Dr. Baggazippian's native tongue.

"Dake zeeks, dake hossfulz. Nach mannera."

He stood up to dismiss Coy Mink, Jr. "Nassa wink," said Dr. Baggazippian, showing Coy Mink, Jr. to the door.

While he had the door open, Dr. Baggazippian called in the next patient, a young man who had been made seasick by the Relax-a-Chair and was soon to vomit.

Coy Mink, Jr. left the Gailor Clinic building and walked across the street to Forrest Park and sat down at the base of the huge bronze equestrian statue of General Nathan Bedford Forrest. General Forrest was buried beneath the statue.

It was three-thirty in the afternoon. Mr. Mink would not be there to take Coy Mink, Jr. home for at least another hour because he always spent the day in an adult movie house and sat through the program twice. Coy Mink, Jr. had found that out by accident. He was routinely riffling the pockets of his father's clothing one afternoon, and came upon a ticket stub: ADMIT ONE. BLUE MOON ADULT CINEMA.

Coy Mink, Jr. considered adult movies another reason why his father had to get it. They were sinful and corrupting and everybody who attended them ought to have their eyes scratched out and then be put to sleep, for good.

Coy Mink, Jr. knew that much about things. He might be crazy, but he knew that much.

Forrest Park is shady in the summertime and there are benches there where even one wearing a black suit and a necktie can sit and be comfortable. Coy Mink, Jr. found such a bench and sat down. After a very short time, he felt himself going to sleep and he shook his head and slapped his own face so he would not. A boy going to sleep in Forrest Park, which was the same as going to sleep in the deep woods, would be slipped up on by a house cat and have his breath taken.

He walked back across the street to the clinic and sat down on the bench in front of it, on a busy street where a house cat was not likely to be roaming and looking for breath to take. Coy Mink, Jr. sat on the bench in front of the clinic for a while then he got up and bought an orange from the crippled black midget, who had brought his wares outside and displayed them on the steps. He took the orange and went back to the bench, but he did not eat it. It would get his fingers sticky if he peeled it and ate it. He put it in his pocket and would wait until he got home to eat it.

There, he could wash his hands, afterwards.

Coy Mink, Jr. took the large container of pills given him by Dr. Baggazippian out of his pocket and looked at them. A young man — wearing sandals, very long hair, and a strange look in his eyes — was passing at that moment. He saw the pills and stopped at the bench.

"You want these?" asked Coy Mink, Jr.

"I never saw any like them before," said the young man. "What kind are they?"

"I don't know. Just peels. Strange writing on them. The doctor just gave them to me. I don't want them. I always throw them away. The Bobble said don't take foreign substances into the body."

The young man took the container, opened it, took out a pill, popped it into his mouth. Then he popped several more. He put the pills in his pocket and walked on, without a word of thanks, as though a large container of pills was just his due.

Coy Mink, Jr. folded his arms and looked straight ahead without blinking his eyes. It would be at least thirty minutes before his father arrived to take him home.

16

Big Rafe Goes to Memphis to See the Roller Board Man

The same Monday morning that Coy Mink, Sr. took his son to Memphis for a visit with the psychiatrist, Big Rafe also went to Memphis, on very important business. This was the day he was scheduled to meet with L. Carlos Biggle, Vice-President for Finance, Roller Board Roadside Inns, and deliver his personal financial statement and the personal financial statements of Tubby and Mona Turmath and Dr. Dennis Dennis, the four being the principals in the corporation formed to obtain a franchise and build and operate a Roller Board Roadside Inn at the Cloverleaf outside Bloat, Mississippi.

About ten o'clock in the morning, Big Rafe locked the door of his office, the one with RAFE MUNGER, LAND DEALS on the window, and got into his late-model Mercury with fancy options and shot out of Bloat, north to Memphis and the national offices of Roller Board Roadside Inns.

Once arrived, Big Rafe approached the lady at the desk outside Biggle's office. "I'm Rafe Munger, Land Deals, Bloat, Mississippi. I've got an appointment with Mr. Biggle."

"Have a seat, Mr. Munger. Mr. Biggle will be with you in a moment."

Biggle's office was one of many in a large basement, underneath an actual Roller Board Inn, with close air, no windows, pink flourescent lighting and a new cut-pile carpet that stored static electricty. Big Rafe got shocked every time he touched anything. Pop! Pop! Pop! It sounded like teeny firecrackers.

The lady at the desk went to the filing cabinet and looked under the "M's" until she found a file labeled "MUNGER, Rafe. Grand Deals." She took it into Mr. Biggle's office and placed it on his desk where he could reach it.

Mr. Biggle was lying on a folding daybed behind his desk, looking up at the Tru-Tone Art print of Jesus on his office wall. All the Roller Board executives had the same picture of Jesus on the walls of their offices. It was company policy, ordered by the founder of Roller Board Roadside Inns, old man Cargo Faircloth, now nearly ninety, who publicly credited Jesus with giving him the idea for stealing the first hundred dollars he ever had in his life, a sum he soon parlayed into the Roller Board empire.

Mr. Biggle was lying on a daybed because he had recently undergone back surgery and needed to stay off his feet.

"Munger?" asked Mr. Biggle. "Munger. Munger. Munger," he repeated, taking the file and hastily looking at it. "Wants a Roller Board franchise, does he? Wants me go over his books, does he? Well, that's my line of business! Send him in!"

"You can go right in, Mr. Munger," said the lady. "Mr. Biggle's office is the last door on your right."

Big Rafe entered the office but he did not see anybody. Biggle, lying behind his desk, was not visible to one entering the office. Mr. Biggle heard Big Rafe and spoke up.

"Mr. Munger? You'll have to excuse me. I've just had back surgery. Got to take it easy."

Big Rafe leaned over the desk and saw Mr. Biggle. "Yes sir!" said Big Rafe, agreeably. He had always found that he could handle any situation by saying "Yes, sir!" in a vigorous, positive way.

"I just got out of the hospital a week ago. Mr. Cargo Faircloth has been mighty good to let me roll this daybed in here, so I can kind of ease the pain."

"Pain? Maybe you should have stayed in the hospital."

"Can't stay off the job too long! In our work, things change so fast, you've got to be here every day, just to keep up."

"Yes, sir!" said Big Rafe.

"Not only that. If a fellow stays off the job too long around here, they'll just set his hat rack out in the hall. If you get what I mean."

"Well, I won't keep you. I've got the financial statements I was supposed to bring you."

Big Rafe handed Mr. Biggle the three financial statements, all in matching blue covers. They were "unaudited personal financial statements with year-end Profit and Loss" and had been prepared by Ealy Nightrose, a Public Accountant in Port Spuds, Mississippi. Mr. Biggle took the statements and looked at the net worth indicated on each.

"Hum! Million! Million and a half! Seven hundred and fifty thousand! Very impressive net worth, here!"

"I don't mind saying, Mr. Biggle, that you're dealing with the big money of Bloat, Mississippi!"

None of the principal were worth anything like the figures shown on their financial statements. Everything was inflated. For instance, Big Rafe inflated his net worth by about three hundred thousand dollars by describing a tract of farm land as a shopping center "under construction." He had also added ten thousand dollars to the value of each of ten rent houses he owned in Bloat, houses not worth four thousand dollars each on the open market.

The Turmaths, Tubby and Mona, had done the same thing. They were actually worth about eight hundred thousand dollars but they made it a million and a half by inflating the receivables due the newspaper and the funeral home, and by inflating the market value of their real estate and such things as "Goodwill" at the funeral home.

Mona Turmath owned stock in her late father's munitions factory in Alabama and they showed it at a greatly inflated "fair market value" on their statement. The stock was almost worthless since the factory no longer manufactured munitions and had just about closed up, except for the part that made children's garden tools.

Dr. Dennis Dennis more or less told the truth on his financial statement, except that he had inflated the amount of his receivables by about three thousand percent, failed to list a seven-year mortgage on his dental equipment, inflated the value of his home in Bloat, Mississippi, and listed under "Assets" six hundred thousand dollars' worth of stock in the telephone company, which he did not have. His wife's parents had it. She was an only child. He would probably have it, one day. What the lawyers did not get.

Mr. Biggle continued to look at the statements, while lying on his back. Once in a while, he winced.

"Can't you get some painkillers for that back?" asked Big Rafe.

"Don't want them! I might become an addict! That's how dope fiends start, taking dope prescribed for pain after surgery. I read about it in *Readers Digest*. How long do you think they'd let me stay on around here if I was a dope fiend? No, sir! No dope for me! I'll just fight it out!"

Mr. Biggle was looking at the Turmaths' statement.

"Who prepared this statement? Who's Ealy Nightrose? CPA?"

"Ealy, he's just a Public Accountant. Ole Miss boy. He's the best in Titus County."

"Mr. and Mrs. Turmath claim to be worth a million and a half. They show stock in something called 'AB and D Company,' listed at nearly half a million. 'AB and D Company' — What's that?"

"That's stock in her late daddy's bidness. He was the founder of Alabama Bomb and Dagger. Made a bundle during World War II. About ten years ago, they went over to plastics. Make lawn furniture, toys. Yes, sir! AB and D is a moneymaker! Mrs. Turmath's brother, another Ole Miss boy, he's the general manager. Takes home about sixty thousand a year!"

"Sixty thousand a year, eh?" said Mr Biggle, giving the statements another glance.

Big Rafe twisted nervously in his chair. Barton Mutt did not make sixty thousand dollars a year. Last time Big Rafe heard, Barton Mutt was on Food Stamps.

"Mr. Munger, I'm no fool! These figures are greatly inflated!"

"Well, sir ... "

"Even so, there does seem to be money here."

"Does that mean we get the franchise?"

"What about morals? Do these partners of yours have good morals, all up and down the line?"

"Yes, sir!"

"In that case, I can guarantee you a franchise. I'll send you a letter of intent in a few days. You can borrow working capital on the strength of it."

"That's mighty good news!" said Big Rafe.

As Big Rafe was leaving Mr. Biggle's office, the lady at the desk stopped him and said:

"Mr. Munger, you have a telephone call on line one."

It was the Executive Vice-President of Roller Board Roadside Inns, calling from his plush office in a nearby building.

"Rafe, I've been looking high and low for you! I've arranged for you to have lunch today with Toy Goodman. Toy's our National Food and Beverage Director. You'll need to meet with him if you want to get all the facts on dining rooms. Toy's waiting right now, upstairs from where you are, in the new Buccaneer Room."

"Lunch?"

"We think of everything at Roller Board Roadside Inns!"

"Yes, sir!"

"How's that boy of yours, Rafe, Jr.? I see by my calendar that he's getting married this Saturday."

At their first meeting, two months ago, Big Rafe had impulsively invited the Executive Vice-President to attend the wedding.

"Rafe, Jr.? He's doing fine! A crackerjack! Ole Miss boy, you know. Made Mr. Reb! Got put up for Mr. Popularity!"

"I'll be there for the wedding," said the Executive Vice-President.

"You don't need to bother coming all the way down to Bloat, just for that!"

"Nonsense, Rafe! We here at Roller Board Roadside Inns consider ourselves one big family. I could no more let the son of a franchise holder get married without my being there than I could miss my own daughter's wedding! I love weddings! Yes sir, I'll be there!"

"We'd love to have you," said Big Rafe.

"Me and the missus. Maybe Mr. and Mrs. Maybath Riddle, too. Maybath, he's our Public Relations Director. He'd love to come and maybe take pictures for the *Roller Board Round-Up*. That's our monthly magazine. Ask Miss Sputts to give you a copy before you leave."

Big Rafe had not planned on having lunch with Toy Goodman. He had wanted to do his business at the Roller Board offices in a hurry so he could drive on into town, to the Blue Moon Adult Cinema. Drat! Lunch with some Food and Beverage Director would kill an hour! Hour and a half!

Toy Goodman was a young man who always wore a poplin suit and vest, with a large gold PRIDE pin in his lapel, indicating he had attended extensive training sessions at Roller Board University and had passed courses in POSITIVENESS, REALIZATION, IDEALIZATION, DETERMINATION and ENERGIZATION.

Goodman grabbed Big Rafe's hand and squeezed it hard. He had once coached high school ball and was flying to Bombay, India, on business, that very afternoon.

Goodman showed Big Rafe through the Buccaneer Room. Its walls were hung with weathered ship's gear, block and tackle, ropes, masts, sextants, treasure chests, flintlock pistols, cutlasses and life-size statues of pirates, all in natural-color pressed Textra-Last plastic.

"The Beef Stroganoff is excellent, today," said Goodman, and he ordered a portion for Big Rafe.

Soon, a plate of Beef Stroganoff, with a spiced apple ring and potato chips, was set before him. Big Rafe tasted it.

"This is good! he said.

"Isn't it?" agreed Toy Goodman.

"You make this here? Can we have food this good at Bloat?"

"All our entrées are prepared at a factory in Leopard Eye, Tennessee. Every one is portion-controlled, packaged in boilproof plastic bags, flash-frozen and shipped to every Roller Board kitchen in the world. When it's time to serve, it's heated in a radar oven. If you have anyone in Bloat with enough sense to operate a radar oven, then you can have food as good as this."

Big Rafe though at minute to himself.

Who the hell was there down there who *could* be trusted to operate a radar oven?

Toy Goodman took Big Rafe on a tour of the kitchen and showed him the massive radar ovens that could warm up over six hundred portions at the same time.

Big Rafe managed to get away from him after about two hours and headed into town, to the Blue Moon Adult Cinema.

17

Mr. Mink Goes to the Blue Moon Adult Cinema

After letting his son out of the car in front of the Gailor Clinic, Mr. Mink drove around the corner to the Steak and Egg Kitchen and had a second breakfast.

He sat at the counter and ordered two scrambled eggs, two sausage patties, buttered toast, hash brown potatoes and coffee.

It came to nearly four dollars, plus tip. That was one bad thing about Memphis. It cost like the mischief to eat breakfast.

Mr. Mink drove out to Sears, walked through Hardware, priced a package of quarter-inch screw eyes, then drove over to Fred Montesi's Supermarket in midtown and brought groceries for a week.

By then, it was nearly noon.

On his way out to the Blue Moon Adult Cinema, Mr. Mink stopped at Pampa's Eat Shop for a barbecue.

Since he had been coming in over a year, Mr. Pampa and his two sisters, who worked the counter, knew him by sight and knew he was from Mississippi.

Mr. Mink did not tell them he came to Memphis every week to

take his son to a psychiatrist. He told them he came to town once a week to buy groceries.

"They don't have any big grocery stores at home. Only the Chinaman's and he's as high as a cat's back."

Mr. Mink had one chopped brown barbeque, a Nu-Grape and two fried peach pies. Two was the limit. There was a sign on the wall that said so. That was all they would let you have, there was such a demand.

"We've got to be fair to everybody," said Mr. Pampa.

Mr. Pampa listened to Gospel music all day long and was very fat. He was always on or off Weight Watchers.

Mr. Mink got to the Blue Moon Adult Cinema about one o'clock.

They had a double feature advertised: "*Bike Bum's Baby* and *Sin Sunday.*"

As soon as Mr. Mink got inside the theatre and looked at the screen, he realized he had already seen the feature that was showing. It was neither *Bike Bum's Baby* nor *Sin Sunday. Sailor's Bitch* was the name of it and he had seen it last week and it was no damn good!

It was another one of those whip pictures.

Whip pictures are all alike! Fakes! Cotton whips. Black cotton fabric stuffed with cotton batting. What they need, those dirty movie houses, is a *real* whip picture!

Sailor's Bitch was finally over and the next feature came on.

Well, toot!

It was *Motel Momma Gets the Hots*. Mr. Mink had seen that one last week, too!

Damn that Blue Moon, to advertise one thing and run another!

Motel Momma was boring. It had been boring the first time he'd seen it.

The people who make adult movies never know when to cut a scene. They will show the same scene on the screen for as long as three minutes. No sense of pace, those people. They knew nothing about action!

Mr. Mink stopped watching the screen and dozed a minute in his seat. Then he looked at his watch. Did he have time to drive out on Lamar Avenue to the Hot Fox Adult Cinema and catch their bill?

Not really. He had to pick up Coy Mink, Jr. in about an hour and a half.

Motel Momma was finally over and they started showing the previews of coming attractions. Mr. Mink had learned from experience that the Blue Moon would never, ever actually show any of the movies previewed as coming attractions. You might see one that looked good in the previews and keep an eye out for it on the screen, but they would never run it.

That was company policy.

Mr. Mink sat through the previews of six coming attractions, all of which bored him. They all had bad sound and looked homemade. Which they were, if he only knew it.

The seventh preview of a coming attraction hit the screen. It was called *Whip Kitten* and the star was Yvonne Hangman.

Yvonne Hangman! The Toast of Bloat!

Mr. Mink was stunned. Yvonne Hangman, the little girl who grew up down the street from him, who used to babysit Coy Mink, Jr., who had gone through all the chairs at the Rainbow Girls...

She had been Flo Ella Dermon, then. Was that really her? He looked closely. It was her, all right! He would know her face anywhere!

So, Yvonne Hangman was making dirty movies.

What a shock, and her supposed to be coming up so big in regular movies, the kind you take wives to see. She must be doing it for the money.

The preview of *Whip Kitten* ended and they started to show *Sailor's Bitch* again.

Mr. Mink quickly got bored again and looked around the theatre. Rafe Munger was sitting two seats down, to his right. Big Rafe. Rafe Munger Land Deals.

What a day for surprises!

Big Rafe waved to Mr. Mink, then got up and moved over to sit down beside him.

"Did you see who was playing that *Whip Kitten*?" asked Big Rafe.

"Did I? I sure did see! Yvonne Hangman!"

"I'll bet you never thought we'd live to see that girl stork naked on the silver screen!"

"I would never have! Ain't it great, the way things have opened up!"

"I'll say it is!" said Big Rafe.

Big Rafe looked around him and over his shoulder, then cleared his throat.

"You never saw me here and I'll the same for you!"

Mr. Mink agreed and the two men sealed the promise with the Masonic handshake.

When Mr. Mink got back to the Gailor Clinic, Coy Mink, Jr.

was sitting on a bench in front of the building, looking neither to the right nor left.

He got in the car and they started home to Bloat.

"How was it with the doctor, today?" asked Mr. Mink.

"All right."

"Did he help you any?"

"I guess."

They drove on a while.

"Did he give you any pills? That doctor?"

"No. No peels."

"Don't they ever give you any pills? Anything to take?"

"Never do," said Coy Mink, Jr. "Never give me any peels."

He took the orange out of his pocket, bit into it, and ate it — pulp, seeds and all.

18

Tuesday: Yvonne Hangman is Coming Home for the Wedding

Davy Sue knocked on the front door of the home of Mrs. Birdie Dermon, mother of the famous Hollywood starlet, Yvonne Hangman.

"Come in, Davy Sue!" said Mrs. Dermon, when she opened the door. "You all set for the wedding?"

Mrs. Dermon was a plain woman with tiny eyes and high blood pressure. People always wondered where Yvonne Hangman had got her looks.

"That's what I'm here about, the wedding," said Davy Sue. "I sent an invitation to Yvonne at that address you gave me and here it is, come back, 'Addressee Unknown.' I don't have time now to get an invitation to her."

"Let me see that," said Mrs. Dermon, taking the envelope from Davy Sue's hand. She looked at the address. "That's where she's supposed to be, all right."

"It won't be the same without my best friend at the wedding!" said Davy Sue.

"Well, don't you worry, Davy Sue, honey. She called long

distance last night, just to chat, and I told her about the wedding and she vowed she'd be here if she had to thumb it the whole way!"

Mrs. Dermon was disabled from high blood pressure, diabetes and phlebitis. If she stood up at all, her left leg would swell up in a strut. She got a little check every month from Social Security and Yvonne sent her money, regularly, or so she said: *Maybe it's a hundred dollars, or maybe only fifty, but it's regular, ever week. Or thereabouts.*

"So Yvonne moved again," said Mrs. Dermon, half to herself. "That's the third or fourth time she's moved this year without telling me."

She pronounced it "Y-vonny." Mrs. Dermon did not know any better. She had lived in Bloat, Mississippi all her life and knew nothing about foreigner's names. Before Flo Ella Dermon became Yvonne Hangman, the most unusual name Birdie Dermon had ever heard was "Hilda" and it was on a plumber's wife. Wilhelm and Hilda Krautz, from over in Coldwater, and both of them full-blood Germans and just as mean as the Devil!

Mrs. Dermon sat down in her living room.

"You notice these floors is clean enough to eat off of," she said. "Even though I'm disable to work, I still keep my house clean!"

Her bed was in the next room. It had three mattresses on it and was made up with a rag doll resting on the pillows. If there was ever a bed high off the ground, it was hers. It would be the end of her, if she ever rolled over at night and fell out of it.

"That Yvonne!" said Mrs. Dermon. "Busy, that's what! Too busy to change her address! Probably moved up to a better apartment! Probably moved to the Coast! She's just too busy!"

"What's Yvonne doing now, Mrs. Dermon? I don't think I've seen her picture in a movie book inside the last three years!"

"She signed for that deal with Pimberg on the Coast, you know!"

Mrs. Dermon talked like the columns of *Variety*, to which she subscribed.

"Blackfeldt at MCA was after her to sign with Delphi Productions, on a percentage, thirty one and five eights after the first three million, or one per cent of the gross on the front end, but she always wanted to work with that Swede, Bergman, so she didn't sign, thinking he would sign her to play Joan of Arc. The Swede, that is. He never asked her, so she opened her own production company, Hangman Arts, and is under option to film the next big hit on the ABC network. It could mean millions. The William Morris Agency is in on it and Carlton Claymore is going to be her next leading man.

"They're talking about having an Yvonne Hangman festival over at Port Spuds at the Nut Theatre. All the early hits, *Moonshiner's Daughter, Moonshiner's Sweetheart* and *Daughter of a Moonshiner*. All her great ones!"

Mrs. Dermon was eager to talk show business. Most people avoided her because she would talk your arm off about Yvonne.

"You know, I always said I wished Yvonne had stayed here and finished high before leaving for Hollywood, but there was no telling her! When she took a notion to go, she just went! Went off with that boy that was working at the radio station, wasn't even a disc jockey, just some kind of announcer, that's all he was!

"Ever time she writes home, she asks about her friends, especially you, Davy Sue. I told her last time I wrote about Miss Effie Chad Reed retiring. Yvonne never had Miss Effie, she was not one to work in an office, but I'm sure she knew her.

"She's just dying to get here for your wedding! I sent her the announcement when it came out in the *Tomcat*. I wish she'd get married. A nice church wedding, right here in Bloat. I'll bet it'd make *Photoplay* magazine!"

Davy Sue could tell Mrs. Dermon was getting ready to talk her arm off. "I'm supposed to meet Big Rafe at the *Tomcat* office!" she interjected. "I'm late now! If you hear anymore from Yvonne about what time she's going to get in, let me know!"

"If you gotta hurry off, you gotta! Mr. Big Rafe won't stand waiting! But you come back! I want to tell you about Yvonne's role coming up that's going to draw her the Academy Award!"

19

Wednesday: Davy Sue, Rixie Leaptrot and Bunny Go to Memphis

"Don't let me forget to stop at the Zoo and see if they found Daddy Merkle's teeth," said Davy Sue.

It was nine-thirty in the morning. Davy Sue, Rixie Leaptrot and Bunny were on the highway, heading north to Memphis.

Daddy Merkle had been at the Zoo several days ago, and while watching the seals, leaning over the rail and laughing at their antics, his upper plate fell right out of his mouth and sank to the bottom of the twenty-foot pool, before he knew what was going on. His upper plate had been loose for years but he had no money to spend on luxuries like Poly-Grip.

Davy Sue had called the Zoo Man and told him about it, right when it happened, but the Zoo Man had just been spurred by a Redtail Hawk and, as he was bleeding profusely at the wrist, had had no time to get the details.

Later, the Merkles found another Zoo Man who promised he would mail the false teeth home, the next time the pool was drained. That had been at least ten days ago, and still no teeth.

Daddy Merkle was not about to stand up with his daughter at

the wedding with no teeth in his mouth!

"I don't know where the Zoo is," said Rixie Leaptrot. "You'll have to show me."

He was driving Big Rafe's Mercury with the fancy options. The three were going to Memphis to pick up tuxedos for Rixie Leaptrot and Bunny to wear at the wedding.

"I'll show you the Zoo, easy enough," said Davy Sue. "I know Memphis like I know Bloat."

It was true. She knew the name of every street in Memphis, where they were on a map and with what streets they intersected. She could tell you the name of every business house on Poplar Avenue, from the Mississippi River east to Interstate 40. It was a gift, something connected with her ability to add a column of figures quicker than a machine. You could put Davy Sue Merkle down in the middle of Memphis blindfolded and she could find her way to anywhere you wanted to go.

She also knew the location of every McDonald's hamburger place, every Krystal, every Whopper Burger outlet, every Kentucky Fried Chicken, every Tops Barbecue in the city.

With Davy Sue Merkle in your car, you were never more than a block away from fast food.

Bunny was asleep in the back seat.

"Why can't he talk, Rixie? Is it something he was born with? Ain't there nothing to be done? No operation? Nothing like that?"

"I don't know, exactly," said Rixie Leaptrot. "I been knowing Bunny two years, now. We met in Arkansas . . . er . . . while working for the State. Highway Department. I never exactly heard anyone say what it is wrong with him. Except for not being able to talk, he's perfect. Just as fine as fella as they come."

"Maybe someone could pay to have him put right," said Davy Sue. "Maybe Big Rafe would, or maybe he could find out who might pay. Maybe the Welfare would."

"Somebody ought to be able to fix him up, seems to me," said Rixie Leaptrot.

They got to the Zoo and looked up the man Davy Sue had told about the teeth. His hand was bandaged where the Redtail Hawk had spurred him.

"I'd a thought you'd a'had them teeth by now, little lady," he said to Davy Sue. "I put them on the Greyhound bus, parcel express, three days ago."

"Well, they ain't showed up," said Davy Sue. "I been checking ever time the mail runs, and ever Greyhound bus that's come through and they ain't been on any of them."

The man left to check his records. He came back with an aluminum clipboard, some shipping forms and bills of lading.

"Sent them out, to Miss Davy Sue Merkle . . ."

"That's me."

"Davy Sue Merkle, Bloat, Alabama."

"Alabama?" screamed Davy Sue.

"Bloat, Alabama," repeated the Zoo Man.

"You flat-out fool!" she screamed. "It's Bloat, MISSISSIPPI!"

The Zoo Man threw up his hands in embarrassment.

"I knew at the time Bloat, Alabama didn't sound right. Bloat, Mississippi, that's where they were supposed to go. I remember now."

"They were my daddy's teeth and he's just got to have them to stand up with me at my wedding!"

"I'm sure sorry, lady," said the Zoo Man.

"We can go down to the Greyhound Depot and check it out," said Rixie Leaptrot. "They might be down there."

"There probably ain't no such place as Bloat, Alabama," said the Zoo Man. "I'm sure sorry, lady. I guess that Redtail Hawk spurring me along about then must have thrown a kink in my mind. Why, just yesterday, I caught myself putting Winesap apple quarters out for the mink. A mink won't eat a Winesap! I should have known that!"

"Never mind," said Davy Sue. "It's just one of those mistakes."

"I sure am sorry, lady."

"How's your hand?" asked Davy Sue. "Where the bird got you?"

"Redtail Hawk," said the Zoo Man, extending a bandaged hand, swollen and blue at the fingers. "Having a devil of a time with it. May have to lance it!"

"Vinegar poultices," said Rixie Leaptrot. "Slice you a Bermuda onion and put it on the wound, then keep a hot vinegar poultice on it," he said. "It'll draw the misery right out!"

"Vinegar poultices!" said the Zoo Man. "I may have to try that!"

"Be sure you use apple cider vinegar!" said Rixie Leaptrot.

The three, Davy Sue, Rixie Leaptrot and Bunny, drove downtown to the Greyhound Depot and checked at the parcel window.

"It was sent to Bloat, Alabama, in place of Bloat, Mississippi," explained Rixie Leaptrot.

The Parcel Man consulted a big thick book.

"There's no such of a place as Bloat, Alabama," he said.

"What does that mean, then?" asked Davy Sue. "What's become of the teeth?"

"By now, that package has probably been sent to the Dead Parcel Office," he said.

"Where's that?" asked Davy Sue.

"Phoenix, Arizona."

"Phoenix, Arizona!" screamed Davy Sue.

"I could put a tracer on it." The Parcel Man started filling out a form. "What was in the package?"

"Teeth. My daddy's false teeth. The uppers."

The Parcel Man entered "Upper Teeth" on a line.

"If you don't hear from us in six months, you can file a claim."

"We'll never again see Daddy Merkle's teeth," said Davy Sue. "I just know it."

Something came over Bunny and he picked up a two-wheel dolly with a steamer trunk on it and held it over his head.

"Here, buddy!" said the Parcel Man. "You don't have to get hot about it!"

"Bunny, put down that trunk and dolly!" said Rixie Leaptrot.

"What is he?" asked the Parcel Man. "Are you folks following a show?"

The next stop was McQuiddy's Tux Rentals.

They had two colors — Lime Green and Salmon. Davy Sue had already decided on Lime Green. Her bridesmaids were making their own dresses out of Lime Green batiste and were going to carry Hydrangeas, dyed green with food color.

They tried to fit Bunny first. He was an odd size, being twenty-eight in the waist and thirty-eight in the chest.

Swayne McQuiddy, who ran the shop and had two branches in Nashville, had run into this before.

"No problem at all!" he said. "No problem at all, for an experienced fitter like me!"

He took the coat from one tux and the pants from another and got a perfect fit. The colors were not exactly the same, however. Bunny's coat was a little lighter than the pants. Beside the coat, the pants looked like Split Pea instead of Lime Green.

"No one will notice, in the excitement," said Mr. McQuiddy. "Besides, it's always dark at dances."

"They're for a wedding," said Davy Sue. "An afternoon wedding, in the bride's home at Bloat, Mississippi."

"Oh!" said Mr. McQuiddy.

He looked at the Lime Green tuxedo and at his three customers.

"Show people?" he asked. "Rock music? Gypsies?"

"This little lady here is marrying the son of the richest man in town," said Rixie Leaptrot.

"Well, I'll be!" said Mr. McQuiddy. "A real wedding! A real Delta wedding!"

Mr. McQuiddy found a shirt for Bunny, made of mocha-colored nylon, with a big bunch of ruffles down the front and a black bow tie, a black satin one, each side as big as a pie plate and fuzzy like a tarantula.

Rixie Leaptrot was easy to fit. He was a size thirty-four regular.

"What about a hat?" he asked. "Don't a hat go with it?" He picked up a green satin high hat and tried it on and looked at himself in the mirror. Rixie Leaptrot was very pleased by his appearance.

"Don't that beat all?" he asked.

Mr. McQuiddy took the hat away from him.

"You don't wear a hat with a tuxedo!" he said. "Those hats are for a black gospel group. They rent costumes from us."

"A man ought to wear a hat if he's dressed up," said Rixie Leaptrot.

"If you really want a hat, I've got some black vinyl Derbies," said Mr. McQuiddy.

"A Derby might look all right," said Rixie Leaptrot.

"They're more for Halloween, though, than a wedding," said Mr. McQuiddy.

"I guess I'll skip a hat, then," said Rixie Leaptrot, "if that's all you got."

Mr. McQuiddy started writing up the rental.

"Fact is," he said, "almost all of our business comes from colored high schools. Frat parties, senior proms, things like that." He sidled up close to Rixie Leaptrot and half whispered in his ear, "Fact is, you folks are the first white people I've seen in here in four, five years."

As a token of his best wishes, he threw in, at no charge, the evening slippers, brown three-quarter length engineer boots made of 100% vinyl, with a zipper on the side for easy getting-on-and-off.

Davy Sue paid him with a check from Big Rafe and said they would have the tuxedos back, first thing Monday.

Mr. McQuiddy followed them to the door, where he grabbed Bunny's hand and shook it vigorously.

"Yes, sir!" he said. "I want you folks to know, it makes me mighty proud to be dressing the groom in a Delta wedding!"

The tuxedos having been rented, boxed, and safely stowed in the car, the three stood in front of McQuiddy's Tux Rentals and watched traffic go by. It was a glorious day, with the air just slightly tainted by automobile exhaust.

"What'll we do now?" asked Davy Sue. "We got all the rest of the day."

Bunny tugged at Rixie Leaptrot's sleeve and when he had his attention, made several quick movements with his hands.

"Bunny says, let's have a picnic!" said Rixie Leaptrot.

"We can get a sack of tacos and go to Overton Park with them!" said Davy Sue. "We can have a picnic and swing on the swings!"

They hit six fast-food stands in the heart of town and by the time they reached Overton Park, they had sacks of Krystal Burgers, tacos, burritos, Shoney's Big Boys, French fries, shakes, Cokes, doughnuts, pizzas, chili dogs, a tub of Colonel Sanders' fried chicken and a dozen fried peach pies, all of it on Big Rafe, who had given Davy Sue thirty dollars for expenses.

By late afternoon, they were stuffed.

Rixie Leaptrot and Davy Sue sat at a picnic table. Bunny was asleep under a tree twenty feet away. Davy Sue was drawing circles with her finger in a pool of spilled Coke. Rixie Leaptrot noticed she looked different. She looked a little worried.

"What's the matter, Davy Sue?"

"Nothing's the matter!"

"I know better!"

"Aw, Rixie, I'm just sort of mixed up!"

"About getting married?"

"How'd you know?"

"I just knew."

"Now that it's time to get married, I just don't know. You know what I mean?"

"Meaning nothing by it, but I can't figure out why a nice girl like you would ever even want to get married to a boy like that Rafe, Jr. He's just flat no-count!"

"I know he is, Rixie. I know he's no-count, but, Rixie, he's RICH! Rixie, I been poor all my life. I've seen my momma and daddy poor all their lives. I've seen everybody poor too long to let something like Rafe, Jr. being no-count stop me from marrying him."

"Does Rafe, Jr. want to get married?"

"Why, no! His daddy told him it would be a good idea. Rafe, Jr. does what Big Rafe says. Big Rafe thinks it would be a good idea for me to marry into the family since I got such a good head for figures. I thought it was a good idea, too — at first. I figured Rafe, Jr. might straighten up, and me and Big Rafe could spend all the time getting richer. That's what I thought, at first. I never expected nothing like love, or anything like that. All I had in mind was getting on Easy Street while I was young. You don't blame me for that, do you?"

"Not one bit," said Rixie Leaptrot. "That's all I've ever been on the lookout for, myself. Easy Street. A rich widow."

"That seemed the thing to do, get on Easy Street, up until lately. Up until I met you and Bunny."

They both looked over at Bunny, still asleep under the tree.

"You don't need to tell me any more," said Rixie Leaptrot. "I know what's in a young girl's heart."

"You do, Rixie?"

"I do!"

"What is it?"

"Sex!"

"Oh, Rixie, what am I to do? You been around. What am I to do?"

"That's easy. Marry Rafe, Jr. for his money and see Bunny on the side!"

"I can't do that. That'd be wrong. That'd be a sin!"

"If it was me, that's what I'd do!" said Rixie Leaptrot.

Davy Sue fished around in the tub of Colonel Sanders' fried chicken and found a little bit of wing. She nibbled alternately on it and a fried pie.

"You got a tapeworm!" said Rixie Leaptrot.

Davy Sue put her head on Rixie's shoulder and started crying.

"What am I going to do, Rixie?"

Rixie patted her shoulder. "We'll think of something," he said.

She straightened up and dried her eyes.

"We've got to start home," she said, and ran on ahead to the car.

Rixie Leaptrot awakened Bunny and they started for the car.

"Bunny, that girl's got the hots for you."

Bunny made an awful face and some very quick movements with his hands.

"I *know* you don't like girls!" said Rixie Leaptrot.

Bunny made some more faces and some more quick movements.

"I *know* you can't stand them!" said Rixie Leaptrot. "I just thought, since she looks so much like a boy, you might be interested."

Bunny made some more awful faces and struck the palm of his hand with his fist.

"OK. Forget it!"

Bunny relaxed and smiled.

"I just don't want you to act a fool with Davy Sue, like you did with that nurse in North Little Rock!"

Bunny hung his head and made a slow, graceful motion with his hand.

"I *know* you're sorry about that, now. But what about that nurse?"

Bunny made two graceful sweeps with his hands.

"All she wanted was a little hug and kiss!"

Bunny made a sweet face.

"And now, for the rest of her life, her nose is going to be setting crooked on her face!"

20

Wednesday: Big Rafe Visits the Stucco Brothers

While Davy Sue, Rixie Leaptrot and Bunny were in Memphis, picking up tuxedos, Big Rafe drove out to the Cloverleaf in his wife's car and called on the Stucco brothers.

Angelo and Dominic Stucco were tomato farmers. They raised Break-O-Day Pinks and Big Boy Reds, which they sold by the thousands to a wholesale produce house in Memphis. During the picking season, the Stucco brothers sometimes had over a hundred men on the payroll.

They furnished each picker a pair of pants with screen wire sewn in the legs, to protect them against snake bites. The snakes were fierce, in among the tomato vines. Hog vipers, bush rattlers and swamp moccasins lay everywhere, sunning among the plants, hoping to catch the long green caterpillars that feed upon tomato leaves. Screen-wire pants and snakeproof gloves were issued to every tomato picker.

Still, every day or so, a tomato picker would get bit on the ankle and his toes would swell up.

Dominic Stucco had come to the United States from Brescia,

Italy, when he was twenty years old. He sent for his brother Angelo two years later and by the time the two men were in their early thirties, they owned over three thousand acres of Mississippi farmland.

The State of Mississippi had to pay them three million dollars for the land used when it put through the Interstate Highway. The Cloverleaf Interchange, which covered over two hundred acres, lay less than half a mile from the Stucco brothers' residence. Some said there was politics involved.

The Stucco brothers were fixed for life, with all that money, especially since both were already up in years, with their families raised.

Angelo was a widower, with seven children and forty-one grandchildren living in Memphis and New Orleans. Dominic had five children and thirty-six grandchildren and had been decorated by the Knights of Columbus. Eighty-nine direct descendents, each one of whom would sue in the courts to get his share, and more, when the old men died.

The estate would be tied up for twenty years, and two or three lawyers would end up with every penny of it. As it happened, one of Angelo's sons *was* a lawyer in Memphis, specializing in garnishments and personal injury suits.

The Stucco brothers had consulted him when Big Rafe first came around, a year ago, talking a land deal that would see a Roller Board Roadside Inn built on their property.

"Big Rafe, he's a crook!" said Angelo to his son.

"You gotta be a crook, Poppa, to make big money!" said the Memphis lawyer, whose name was Jerome Stucco.

On Jerome's advice, the Stucco brothers gave Big Rafe an option to buy one hundred acres of land for the motel, and a proposed shopping center, and in exchange took his personal check for twenty-five thousand dollars as a down payment, with the understanding that they would not deposit it until Big Rafe gave them the word.

Now, Big Rafe's application for a Roller Board Roadside Inn franchise had been approved, on the basis of inflated financial statements. Soon, he would have the formal letter of commitment. With it, he would be able to borrow construction money and operating expenses from any bank in Memphis and deposit enough of it in his account to cover the check he had given the Stucco brothers for the down payment.

It was going to be close.

It was all just one big paper exchange, with no cash involved — the sort of land deal he had put together, time and again, in the past. It would be close, but he could swing it.

Big Rafe drove up into the driveway of Angelo's house, which adjoined the office of Stucco Brothers Tomato Packers and Shippers.

Angelo Stucco came out to see him.

"Hoddy, Angelo!" said Big Rafe.

"Meester Land Deals!" said Angelo. "You wanta buy tomatoes?"

"Just passing by, Angelo. Thought I'd say hello!"

Angelo nodded a greeting.

"Still holding that check, Angelo?"

Angelo shifted his weight. He had Barker's Gait. "Still holda check. When you letta me deposit?"

"Just a few days, Angelo. Just a few days!"

Angelo took off his straw hat and wiped the sweat band with a handkerchief.

"My son Jerome, he's a lawyer in Memphis. He say I should no holda check any longer. He calla your bank! Your check, itsa no good! He says I should deposit check and if it bounces, sue you!"

Big Rafe's jaw dropped. "Our deal was, that you'd hold the check until I said deposit it. I never figured you, Angelo, to go back on a deal."

"I've helda check for five months. I never thought you would want me to holda so long."

"That check'll be good, Angelo. In a few days, by Monday week. You deposit it, Monday week, if you have to. Go ahead."

Big Rafe was bluffing. Even if he got the letter of commitment tomorrow, it would take him a week, maybe two weeks, to actually raise the money to cover the check.

"Go ahead and deposit it. If you need the money."

Angelo straightened up proudly. "Stucco brothers do not NEEDA the money! My son, the Memphis lawyer, he says I OUGHTA deposit it. He says, we have no deal on the one hundred acres ifa your checka no good. That's all. Stucco brothers do not NEEDA the money! I will hold the check until you say deposit!"

"'Preciate it, Angelo!"

Angelo Stucco forced Big Rafe to accept a big basket of ripe tomatoes before he left.

21

Thursday: Rixie Leaptrot and Bunny Go to the Lawn Party

"There's no way out of it, boys," said Big Rafe. "You've got to go to Toddy Alexander's party. He's planned it for months, ever since Rafe, Jr.'s engagement was announced. Toddy, he was Pledgemaster of Rafe, Jr.'s fraternity at Ole Miss and he's what you might call Rafe, Jr.'s best friend."

"You say this Toddy Alexander's rich?" asked Rixie Leaptrot.

"About as rich as they got around here. Toddy, him and his brothers, Bale and Trim, inherited everything ole man Alexander had: Rosecliff Plantation, ten thousand acres of soy beans, ten thousand acres of cotton, everything. All three boys went to Ole Miss but there's not a one of them can write his own name. They're not weak upstairs, nothing like that, it's just they always had other things besides education on their minds. Parties. Drinking. Trim, he holds the all-time record for drinking fishbowls of beer at the Top Hat in Sardis."

Big Rafe leaned close and said, confidentially, "Between you and me, there ain't enough sense between the three of them to hold that plantation together another year. The old man should have left it to some sort of trustee or guardian, somebody that would manage it for those boys, somebody like me.

"Those Alexander boys, they're going to lose it all, you watch what I say!

"The day after the old man's funeral, the three of them went up to Memphis, to Oak Hall and Julius Lewis and bought ten thousand dollars worth of new clothes, apiece. Five hundred dollars worth of shoes for each, eight or ten pairs.

"Since then, it's been one long party out at Rosecliff. They stop just long enough to catch a little sleep, then get up and party some more!"

"Sounds like Heaven, to me," said Roxie Leaptrot.

"They keep one five-piece dance band or another on the highway between here and Memphis all the time," said Big Rafe.

"Do they know about Rafe, Jr. being in the jailhouse?" asked Rixie Leaptrot.

"Not a word! They think he's been called up. That's what I told Toddy. That's another thing. We been telling people around here that Bunny was a frat brother of Rafe, Jr.'s at Ole Miss. That won't work over at Rosecliff. Everybody there has been to Ole Miss, some of them for as long as seven or eight years. They'll know better!"

"We could say Bunny's a friend from the University of Arkansas," said Rixie Leaptrot. "Mighty fine school. I once worked there, sweeping out the Ole Main."

"They got a Mr. Popularity there?" asked Big Rafe. "A Johnny Reb? Something like that?"

"Reckon they do," said Rixie Leaptrot.

"Rixie, I'm leaving it to you to carry this off! I got a lot riding on it. In fact, if we carry off this wedding, and everything goes smooth with a bidness deal I'm planning, I'll be real grateful to you both. I'll make it worth your while!"

Rixie Leaptrot put out his right hand. "We're your men!" he said, resolutely.

"The Alexanders are sending a car for you tonight," said Big Rafe. "I told them to pick you up at the Mink Motel. Six-thirty. One other thing, I told them Bunny's name was Bunny VAN Whitesides. I added the VAN. I just thought it sounded a little better than plain 'Bunny Whitesides.' By the way, his name is not really 'Bunny,' is it? That 'Bunny' must be just a nickname."

"Far as I know, 'Bunny' is it. His real name," said Rixie Leaptrot. "Me and him, we been on the bum together two years now, and I never picked up no other name. Bunny's people, they was Nazarenes. Nazarenes, or maybe Pennycost, and they think it was God as made him a mute. That's why they run him off. Made him get out! They didn't want no curse of God under their roof!

Bunny's been on his own since he was thirteen."

"And you can talk to him? Understand him? With no trouble?"

"That's because my folks was circus people," said Rixie Leaptrot. "I'm gifted! I can talk to animals, the same way."

Big Rafe frowned.

"That's very interesting," he said. He looked at his watch. "You boys got just an hour to get cleaned up and dressed. Be sure to wear those new clothes I bought you! You want to look nice when you get to Rosecliff."

Rixie Leaptrot and Bunny were bathed, shaved, combed and dressed in their plastic finery when the Alexanders' car, a big, black Spaatz-Imbatta, one of the old ones with the chrome luggage box at the back, called for them at the Mink Motel.

Coy Mink, Jr. threatened to kill the driver, a young black man wearing a sort of chauffeur's uniform, when he asked for Rixie Leaptrot at the desk.

After Rixie Leaptrot and Bunny were in the car and headed toward Rosecliff, the driver turned to them and said:

"That man at the desk, he's crazy! He said he was going to kill me! That man don't even know me!"

"They say not to worry about him," said Rixie Leaptrot. "He's taking treatments."

Rosecliff Plantation was a twenty-minute drive from Bloat. The driver turned off the highway and headed down a private drive lined on both sides with pecan trees, until they came upon an Italian Renaissance mansion, made of marble and bricks and stucco, all painted rose.

A marquee of striped circus canvas had been set up outside on the lawn and was decorated with strings of colored lights in Japanese lanterns. Hurricane lamps, glass chimneys with candles in them, lined the drives and walkways.

Two hundred people had assembled to honor the proxy for Rafe, Jr.

Toddy Alexander, thirty years old, single, tall, heavy, and wearing smoked eyeglasses with tasteful rims, opened the door of the Spaatz-Imbatta and helped Rixie Leaptrot and Bunny get out.

"Toddy Alexander," he said, introducing himself in a deep voice, with a Southern accent that almost seemed artificial. "You must be Bunny!"

He looked Bunny up and down, noting his plastic clothing.

Toddy Alexander was wearing white linen pants, white silk socks, white leather shoes with a red sponge rubber sole, a long-sleeved silk shirt in a colorful floral pattern and a navy blue linen

Toddy Alexander could not write his own name.

blazer with gold buttons.

All the other men there were wearing the same thing. It was what rich Mississippi men wore to summer parties on the lawn.

"VAN Whitesides," said Toddy Alexander, pompously. "VAN Whitesides. I knew some VAN Whitesides over in Columbus. Not the Delta, mind you, but still fine people. Dartmouth VAN Whitesides. Older brother named Flintworth VAN Whitesides. I suppose you must be one of the cousins from around Tunica."

A crowd had gathered at the car to see the proxy. Rixie Leaptrot took over and started working it, like he used to do when he was a sideshow pitchman.

"This here is Bunny Van Whitesides, from Rogers, Arkansas. University of Arkansas man. His daddy, why, his daddy is the biggest chicken grower in the state of Arkansas. Over five million live chickens on his place at any one time."

The crowd was impressed by the figure "five million."

"... and not only that, Bunny here was, six years running, the Poultry Prince of Northwest Arkansas!"

Rixie Leaptrot knew he had them and threw in the clincher.

"... and his sister, Patty Jane, is right now the reigning Miss Pink Tomato of the Warren, Arkansas Tomato Festival!"

Toddy Alexander beamed proudly and clutched Bunny to his bosom.

"It's an honah, suh, to have you among us!" he said.

Toddy Alexander then hugged Rixie Leaptrot in a spirit of camaraderie and put a paper plate of food in his hand.

"Just a little chicken salad and frozen fruit sherbet," he said. "The real dinner will be served later."

Toddy Alexander pointed across the grounds to where a Negro man in a maroon dinner jacket was tending a bed of coals and sopping sauce on two strange-looking pieces of meat.

"Turtle legs," said Toddy Alexander. "We caught a three hundred pound snapping turtle in the river and dressed it out, and we're barbecuing the front legs here tonight. That's my butler, over there, right now, turning it over the coals."

"A butler?" exclaimed Rixie Leaptrot. "I don't believe I've ever been anywhere before where they had a butler!"

Toddy Alexander had good manners. He did not want to make his guest feel ill at ease.

"I say 'butler.' Actually, he's just an old snuff-mouthed coon. Used to be the yardman. But he dearly loves to put on a wool dinner jacket in the summertime!"

Toddy Alexander led his two guests over to the fire, and they looked at the turtle legs.

"They've turned green, them laigs!" said Rixie Leaptrot.

"You've had them too long off the ice!"

A two hundred and seventy-eight pound young woman, with sixty thousand dollars' worth of emeralds on her fingers, a big, flash-toothed carnivore who would eat anything — one of the three fat Robinson sisters from Friars Point — heard Rixie Leaptrot mention green meat and gagged.

"If it tastes like bleach, I'm not going to eat it!" she said.

"It's supposed to be green," said Toddy Alexander, patronizingly.

"If it tastes like bleach, I'm not going to eat it!" she repeated, and left, going back to the river bank, where she had been fishing.

The Okipitta River, a stagnant ribbon of dark water that you could step across in some places, ran through the Alexander estate, not thirty yards from the great house. As diversion for his guests, Toddy Alexander had bought two hundred bamboo fishing poles and had them fitted out with hooks and line. Thirty little colored boys stood at the ready along the banks of the river to bait the hooks and remove the catch.

The guests did not have to dirty their hands.

About fifty of them, dressed in finery bought in Memphis or Greenville, stood along the river, holding champagne glasses and dipping hooks in the river. Once in a while, someone would catch a grunion, a hideous eel with a dog's head and two front legs, or maybe a mud cat or a mush puppy.

One caught a swamp skimmer. When fried in lard, a swamp skimmer makes might good eating.

"Care to fish?" asked Toddy Alexander of Rixie Leaptrot.

"No, thanks. I'll just have some more of this stuff in the glass. Champagne, you say?"

"Just a cheap one," said Toddy Alexander. "What's this nonsense about Rafe, Jr. being called up by the National Guard? Everyone knows he was thrown out of the National Guard for stealing a flamethrower and burning up a nigger rent house and a taxicab. Took a pre-trail pardon from the Governor to keep him out of Parchman, then and there."

"I don't know nothing about that," said Rixie Leaptrot.

"I believe you know more than you're telling! What about Bunny? Why hasn't he said anything to anybody here tonight?"

"Throat trouble," said Rixie Leaptrot. "Growths in his throat!"

A bond daddy from Memphis, newly come to the big money, heard them talking about throat trouble.

"My brother-in-law's got the same thing! Places in his throat. There's nothing you can do for it! I know! He's been to Mayo's."

Toddy Alexander introduced the bond salesman to Rixie Leaptrot.

"This is Duff Lovedale. He's helping me and my brothers invest our ... extra money."

"Municipal bonds," said Lovedale. "I'd like to put you in a few good municipal bonds," he said to Rixie Leaptrot, reverting to the lingo of his earlier calling, used-automobile sales.

"No, thanks," said Rixie Leaptrot, who knew an aluminum-siding salesman when he saw one.

"Where's Bale and Trim?" asked Duff.

Toddy Alexander pointed to the marquee and a man passed out under it, with his head in a washtub of potato salad.

"There's Trim," he said. "Bale's up in his room, drinking. He's in a black mood. A brown study."

"What's bothering him?" asked Duff.

"They took his Tommy gun away from him, that's what! Today, the Federal agents came out here and seized his Tommy Gun. It's really got him down. If there was one thing Bale loved to do, it was go out in the pasture with that Tommy gun and cut a cow in two!"

"That sounds serious!" said Duff. "Won't there be some trouble, with him having a Tommy gun?"

"He'll be indicted, they said. Tried, I suppose. I'll have to fix everything, I guess."

Guests continued to arrive.

One, that madcap Macy Pearl from Grenada, arrived by parachute from a chartered single-engine airplane, something he frequently did if it was a really big party.

Another, a man whose name they never did get, arrived on a motorcycle going a hundred miles an hour. He could not stop in time and plowed right into the wall of the house and flew off the machine and landed thirty feet away, unconscious. Every now and then during the evening, someone would go and try to revive him, but they could not get his helmet off and since it had turned around backwards, there was no way to see his face.

They knew he was supposed to be a guest because he was wearing white linen pants and a blue blazer.

By ten-thirty, everyone had had his fill of barbecued turtle leg, potato salad, baked beans, tuna salad, chicken salad, dressed eggs, pickles, candy, cakes, beer and champagne.

No one was paying any attention to Rixie Leaptrot and Bunny.

At eleven o'clock, Toddy Alexander called for a toast to the bridegroom.

Bale Alexander came out of the house with a pistol around midnight and started shooting out the colored lights.

About one o'clock in the morning, the driver took Rixie Leaptrot and Bunny back to the Mink Motel.

22

Friday: Dr. Dennis Dennis, Dentist, and His Wife at Home

"I don't believe Rafe Munger will ever get a Roller Board Roadside Inn opened up at the Cloverleaf," said Baxter Dennis, Dr. Dennis Dennis' thirty-three year old wife, as she and the dentist sat in the den of their ranch-style house in the newest subdivision in Bloat.

She was from one of those rich east Memphis families that name their daughters "Chapman" or "Ingalls" or "Stinnett," when "Tammy" would do just as well.

"He's had a year already, and he hasn't even turned the first shovelful of dirt!" she said.

Every room in Dr. Dennis' home, including bath, half-bath, kitchen and utility storage, was panelled in Knotty Bamboo, nailed on right over cedar studs. There was no insulation nor fiberglass batts between the paneling and the outside siding.

The house had been built by Rafe Munger.

He built them all that way. That is why he could sell them cheap and that is why they are cold in the winter and hot in the summer.

The house was All-Electric, including room intercom, built-in vacuum cleaner, smoke detector and burglar alarm. Each month, the electric bill was bigger than the house note.

Dr. Dennis and his wife were eating lunch on TV trays and watching on television a brother-and-sister act, in their own variety show.

"That kid can't sing!" said Baxter. "Why do they let him on television if he can't sing?"

"Why do you have to be critical of everything?" asked Dr. Dennis. "Why can't you boost instead of knock?"

Mrs. Dennis uttered a foul oath.

"You didn't use to talk like that," he said. "You didn't talk like that when you were a debutante in Memphis. You were clean-mouthed, then."

Mrs. Dennis repeated the oath, only double.

"I wish you wouldn't talk bad. You didn't use to talk bad."

"That was before you brought me down here to live right cheek-to-cheek with these ignorant rednecks. Having to live in Bloat, Mississippi would make anybody cuss!"

The Dennis home was decorated with Lucite flowers and string sculpture.

"I had to come to where I could make a living, to where there's a world of bad teeth. U.S. Government surveys show there's more bad teeth in a ten-mile circle of Bloat, Mississippi than anywhere else except Appalachia."

Mrs. Dennis scoffed.

"How can you sit there eating chunk tuna and call what you make 'a living'?" she asked. "You don't make enough money to keep me in cocoa butter!"

"I can't figure that out, either," he said. "Here I am, the only dennis in the whole county and, whereas I ought to be making it big, I can barely keep up this house and pay the dennis supply company."

"You're not having to dilute the Novacaine again, are you?" demanded Baxter.

"Now you quit that! I have never once diluted the Novacaine! I don't know how that story got started and I just wish you'd quit bringing it up!"

Baxter Dennis started rubbing suntan oil on her neck.

She laid out in the sun all day long in the summer, getting brown, browner, brownest.

"You going out in the sun again?" asked Dr. Dennis.

"What business is it of yours?" she asked.

"You're already brown as a nigger!" he said.

"When I married you, I thought you were going to be a dennis in Memphis, and you'd make lots of money, and we could live in Fox Meadows and join the University Club and eat at Justine's, and that I could have charge accounts, just like I did when I was living with Miss Ida Faye and Roy Mack."

Miss Ida Faye and Roy Mack.

That was how Baxter Dennis referred to her parents, Ida Faye and Roy Mack Bibbslinger.

Her grandfather had been in World War I and got the Croix de Guerre for being bit on the hip by his own horse, or so the story went.

"... instead, you come down here and be the dennis and I'm stuck in this house all day while you're throwing gold inlays, and me with nobody to talk to but that dumb girl that lives down the road.

"She came over here yesterday and do you know what she said to me? She had all this green stuff in her apron and she said, 'Baxter, you want some OKER?' OKER! That's okra, to us! 'Do you want some OKER?'"

"Did you thank her?" asked Dr. Dennis. He had been brought up right and knew about thanking people.

Baxter threw up her hands and all but washed them of Dr. Dennis Dennis, the dentist.

"I don't know what Roy Mack would say if he knew I signed that false financial statement, saying I owned six hundred thousand dollars of the phone company, just so you could get in with Rafe Munger on a Roller Board Roadside Inn, I swear I don't!"

"All that stock will be yours as soon as your parents pass away," said Dr. Dennis.

"No telling what they've done to their will since I married you! They never did like you! They may have left it all to Billy Graham, just to keep you from getting your hands on it!"

"Don't say things like that! I'm worried enough about this Roller Board deal as it is, without you bringing up something like that!"

"You ought to be worried, lying like you did, and making me lie!"

"I never told a lie or turned in a false statement in all my borned days, until now!"

"Why'd you do it, then, if you had such a perfect record?"

"I had to! It's the only way we're ever going to have any money. If that Roller Board Roadside Inn gets going, it'll mean we pick up a hundred thousand dollars a year. At the minimum!"

"You just better not ever let Roy Mack find out I lied on a financial statement!" said Baxter.

She poured a Bloody Mary from the pitcher in the refrigerator

Baxter Dennis uttered another foul oath.

and started outside with it, to sit in the sun and get browner.

"You're not going to sit out in the sun with that, are you?" asked Dr. Dennis.

"What if I am?"

"If you drink alcohol in the sun, you'll get skin cancer that much quicker!"

"What do you know about medicine, being a mouth plumber!" She uttered another foul oath.

"Why do you have to cuss all the time?" asked Dr. Dennis. "My mother never did cuss."

23

Friday: Davy Sue's Parents at Home

Daddy Merkle sat on his porch reading a tract titled "Moab and the Serpent of the Lord."

Mrs. Merkle, mother of the bride-to-be, was whipping a hem in the dress she was going to wear to the wedding.

"This time tomorrow, our baby girl will be Mizzrizz Rafe Junior Munger," she said.

"Sooner can a camel pass through the eye of a needle than a rich man enter the Kingdom of Heaven," said Daddy Merkle, in a veiled reference to Rafe, Jr.

Daddy Merkle quit rocking and threw down the tract.

"I don't like it!" he said. "It ain't the Lord's way, to have a proxy wedding!"

"Lord's way or not, it's legal!" said Mrs. Munger. "Legal and binding. Davy Sue is going to be the legal Mizzrizz Rafe Junior Munger, entitled to what's his is hers!"

"Covet not thy neighbor's ass or ox!"

"The Bobble don't say nothing about Rafe Munger's money!"

"It's a sin to covet Rafe Munger's money!"

"It'll be Davy Sue's money, when she's married," said Mrs. Merkle. "And she'll pay for an operation to strip these verrycose veins in my legs."

"The Welfare will pay for it, right now! That's what your Welfare worker said, when she came out here to put you on Disabled to Work!"

"I don't want the Welfare to pay for it. I still got my pride, if I don't have nothing else left. My daughter, Mizzrizz Rafe Junior Munger, will pay for it!"

Daddy Merkle picked up a tow sack and went off into the woods behind the house, to get more copperheads for the Sabbath.

24

Friday: The Stucco Brothers Discuss Big Rafe

"This check, itsa never be any good!" said Angelo Stucco. "I just talka to bank. Rafa Munger, he's never have this much money at one time ina his life!"

Angelo Stucco sat at his desk in the tomato shipping building.

Dominic Stucco sat across from him, polishing his Knights of Columbus medals and regalia, in preparation for an Installation and Grand March at the next meeting.

"Whatsa Jerome say?" asked Dominic, as he applied brass polish to an ornamental breast plate.

Jerome was his nephew who practiced law in Memphis and sued a lot of schoolteachers on behalf of the Thrift Loan and Thrift Company.

Any loan company will lend money to a schoolteacher. A lot of schoolteachers owe four or five loan companies at the same time and sooner or later they get in too deep, and miss their payments to Thrift Loan and Thrift, and Jerome sues them and levies a garnishment on them. Three garnishments and a schoolteacher gets fired, even if he has tenure.

Tenure will not protect a teacher who is guilty of moral turpitude, and that is what being garnished three times amounts to, according to Mr. Arson Croneburger, the school board's legal advisor.

"Jerome, he says deposit the check," said Angelo. "When it comesa back, we sue Rafa Munger for one million dollars!"

"Munger'sa no good," said Dominic. "I hope he goesa to jail!"

"He belongs in jail!" said Angelo. "Butta, I gotta better idea!"

"Killa him?"

"No killa him!" said Angelo. "Thatsa the old daysa! This idea I gotta isa smart idea!"

"Break his legs?" asked Dominic. "We call Grillo, Guido and Giovanni anda they break his legs?"

"Break legs isa out! Woulda smart lawyer lika Jerome break somebody'sa legs? No! Jerome would use his head! I'ma use my head! Why does Rafa Munger wanta our land? To build Roller Boarda Motel! Right! Why? Becausa Roller Boarda Motel make money! Lotsa money! Why shoulda we help Rafa Munger make lotsa money?"

"No gooda reason!" said Dominic.

"We shoulda make the money! We shoulda own motel!"

"Lotsa hard work, runna motel," said Dominic.

"How hard can ita be? You open up and whena somebody drives in and wantsa rooma, you letta them have it!"

"Have to clean up after them!"

"We hire lottsa niggers to cleana up! We take it easy! We go to conventions, inna Memphis. Get lottsa wine, lottsa pasta!"

"How much we have to pay niggers to cleana up?" asked Dominic.

"Forty dollars a weeka!"

"Two times what we pay tomato pickers?"

"Dominic, this isa modern daysa! We have to pay bigga money to getta help."

"How we getta Roller Boarda Motel?"

"I'ma go to Memphis this afternoon, to finda out. I'ma take Rafa Munger's check up therea today, to the topa man, tella him Rafa Munger'sa no good. We own land, we shoulda get the franchisa!"

"To hell witha Rafa Munger!" said Dominic.

"We will getta the franchise!" said Angelo.

"They don't know us! Mighta just laugh at you!"

Angelo Stucco opened his wallet and showed Dominic

Stucco another check.

"Thisa check made out to Roller Boarda.One halfa million dollars! Cashier'sa check! I gotta from bank this morning! Roller Boarda not know Stucco Brothers, butta they know cashier'sa check, whena they see it."

25

Friday: Things Become Too Much for Brother Pond

Brother Pond, the fifteen-year-old ordained Baptist minister who was going to perform the wedding ceremony, had stayed upstairs in his room since Sunday afternoon, coming down only for meals.

It was now early Friday morning and his mother, who had been Ramona Chops of Tunica before she married Jack Pond, a "tire builder" at the Firestone plant in Memphis, was getting worried about him and told her husband so.

"I'll tell you what makes me uneasy about Brother Pond," she said. "He just runs through the Blessing when he comes downstairs to eat. He hasn't taken the time and asked a pretty Blessing since last Saturday night. He's sick! He's worried, or sick, or upset, or something."

"He ought to get outside and run in the sunlight," said his father. "It's not good for a boy of fifteen to stay upstairs all the time reading church books!"

"Brother Pond is a preacher now!" said his mother. "He can't just go outside and run wild, like he was a regular boy!"

"That's what he ought to do! Run! There's a man at the plant who runs on his lunch hour instead of eating dinner. Every day, he runs instead of eats. He's brought his pressure down from two-hundred-over-something to a-hundred-fifty-over-something!"

Upstairs, Brother Pond was consulting a ten-volume collection of the sermons of the Reverend C. L. Music of Reptile Springs, Texas.

He had decided last Sunday afternoon that he would not perform the wedding of Davy Sue Merkle and Rafe, Jr., because Rafe, Jr. was a drunkard, a mocker, a rowdy, a prodigal, a whoremonger and worse, and to marry him in the church would be to risk the wrath of the Lord.

Brother Pond was looking in the books for some support for his position but there was nothing on the subject in the works of the Reverend Music, or in the only other book in his library, a five-hundred-page account of Hitler's persecution of the German Lutherans, written in 1948 by one Waldemar Seitzgang.

He had not yet told anyone of his decision. He was putting it off as long as possible because he knew he did not have the strength to stand up to those in Bloat who would not understand, who would curse him and call him a Fool.

His own mother, for instance, would be very difficult about it, since she had bought him a new blue suit from Slipweasel and Drat Mercantile in Port Spuds, and had laid in a dozen boxes of flash cubes to take pictures of him while he tied the knot.

The wedding was less than twenty-four hours away.

Brother Pond was getting desperate.

He had been awake all night, fighting with the Devil and the temptation to go ahead and perform the wedding anyway, simply to avoid conflict.

Brother Buell Mealer had been no help. He had said to go ahead and perform the ceremony and let the Lord worry about straightening out Rafe, Jr. afterwards. Maybe, said Brother Mealer, Davy Sue, herself, would prove to be the instrument of the Lord's work.

"Davy Sue Merkle must have been chosen by the Lord to Save Rafe, Jr.," said Brother Mealer. "There's no other reason I can think of for why she'd be wanting to marry him."

Brother Mealer, Brother Pond now realized, would marry the Devil, if there was a Love Offering in it for him.

At nine o'clock, Brother Pond had another bad attack of chills and shakes and started crying and vomiting.

It was the Devil testing him.

At nine-thirty, he called his mother up to his room and told her he would not perform the ceremony and asked her to notify Davy Sue.

Ramona Pond telephoned Brother Mealer.

"Brother Mealer, you've got to come over here, right away! Brother Pond is having some strange notions!"

By the time Brother Mealer arrived at the Pond house, Brother Pond had gone into some kind of spell. There he was, sitting in a wing chair in the combination bedroom and study that had been furnished by his mother, wearing his Navy blue wool suit, his white shirt with the plastic stays in the collar and his black silk necktie. (It was really rayon but a discount store in Memphis advertised it as silk. They are going to get in trouble, one day.)

The Works of Waldemar Seitzgang was open on the desk in front of Brother Pond.

He had not had his clothes off since he came home from church last Sunday and he smelled to high heaven.

"What's the matter, Brother Pond?" asked Brother Mealer. "Mrs. Pond says that you are not going to perform the wedding ceremony! Brother Pond, that wedding's got to go ahead! There's too much depending on it! I know you don't think Rafe, Jr. is a worthy Christian, but I happen to know his father's got a lot riding on that wedding. This whole town has a lot riding on it!"

Brother Pond started crying. He sobbed and sobbed. Between sobs, he blurted out his love for Bloat and how he did not want to do anything to hurt it.

"The Lord does not want Rafe, Jr. married in the church," he said. "I will not perform the ceremony and risk damnation!"

"I guess I'll have to perform the ceremony, myself," said Brother Mealer. "Davy Sue'll understand, Brother Pond. We all understand."

Brother Mealer left the house, to tell Davy Sue.

Brother Pond sat there, shaking, sobbing, crying, coughing, and vomiting. Saliva drooled from his lips. Brother Pond was only fifteen, but he knew what newly married couples did on their wedding night. He had been ordained two years ago and since then, he had not indulged in self-abuse.

Never! Not once! He was that much of a Christian.

Thinking about the wedding night had unhinged him.

He sat there in his chair, in his filthy clothes, until about noon; then he went crazy.

He burst out of his room, stark naked, screaming at the top of his lungs, and ran outside, down the highway, toward Memphis, dodging semi-trailers every foot of the way. Brother Pond was strong, and fast, too. It took three men to catch him, hold him down and put some clothes on him.

By the time the Spit Cafe put out its supper menu, Brother Pond was strapped to a bed at the Mental Health Center in Oxford, and everybody in Bloat knew it.

They left him there, under the influence of Valium, until nine o'clock that night, when an elderly medical doctor with white hair and a white moustache came in to talk to him.

The doctor released Brother Pond and he sat up in bed.

"I'm too bad to be a preacher," said Brother Pond. "I was born for a rowdy!"

"But the Lord called you!" said the doctor.

"That was then. This is now. I'm born for a sinner. I know that, now!"

"Are you through with the Lord?" asked the doctor.

"No. I'm still His tool. His plaything. Clay in His hands."

"And He's no longer calling you?"

"I don't know. Maybe He still is, maybe in a different way. I've got this funny feeling that I'd like to sell men's shirts. Ties. I like to dress up. I feel better dressed up. I'd like to see everybody dressed up. I'd like to work around clothes. I think that's what the Lord wants me to do."

"You feel the Lord is calling you into the mercantile trades?" asked the doctor.

"I think the Lord is calling me to be the manager of a J. C. Penney store," said Brother Pond.

26

Friday: Tubby Turmath at the Country Club

High noon.

It was high noon, for certain, because they had just blown the noon steam whistle at the axe-handle factory.

Tubby Turmath sat at a table in the Spit Cafe, waiting for Mom to bring him his "dinner." He had enough money to order *a la carte* and did not have to settle for the plate lunch — a meat and three vegetables. Today, he was having breaded veal cutlets and spaghetti, something the cook had to work up special.

Mom brought Tubby the first course, the small Spit Special Salad and he poured half a full bottle of Blue Cheese salad dressing on it and started eating it with buttered crackers.

The small Spit Special Salad was made out of lettuce with a few pieces of tomato and chopped green onions and sprinkled with little pieces of artificial something or other, flavored like bacon and crunchy when you bit them.

Tubby still had some salad left in the bowl when Mom brought the breaded veal cutlets, two of them the size of slices of Wonder Bread, and spaghetti, with meat and tomato sauce.

You talk about a big plate of food, this was it!

Tubby dumped an entire can of Parmesan cheese on the

spaghetti, then started in on it and the cutlets.

When he had finally finished, Mom took away the plate and asked, "You want some dessert today, Mr. Tubby?"

"Gimme a big slice of that coconut custard pie, with a double-dip ice cream."

When Tubby Turmath first showed up in Bloat, years ago, when he was first courting Mona Mutt, whom he had met at a fraternity party, he was called "Bull" Turmath.

After ten years of eating at the Spit, "Bull" had become "Tubby" and now everyone called him that, even to his face.

If he kept eating like he did, it would not be long before he was called "Hippo." Or "Doctor Fats" or "Lard Ass."

Dessert finished, Tubby lingered in the Spit, drinking coffee. He drank four cups, one right after the other, cooling each with a spoonful of crushed ice from his water glass.

Tubby had to drink lots of coffee, these days, just to stay awake.

It was always cool and quiet in the barroom of the Bloat Country Club.

Tubby sat there every afternoon, enveloped in the near darkness, looking out a wide picture window at the swimming pool and the golf course and the highway. He loved to sit and watch the cars go by, far off in the distance, two hundred yards away. When he was not watching the cars, he watched the swimming pool and young Carlena McLathers, as she dived and splashed and ran away from boys.

Carlena, age seventeen, was a freshman at Southwestern at Memphis, a liberal arts college with high academic standards, where they make you pass Bible before you can graduate.

There were some afternoons when Tubby never took his eyes off her.

Carlena had lots of money. She was the only child of old Carl McLathers, who owned, outright, Carl McLathers Chemical Company, the manufacturers of Black Rascal House Paint. Black Rascal was sold all over the South. Fine quality. It would not chip or peel.

Carlena owned over fifty bathing suits.

Tubby had been keeping track of them since about June fifteenth and he had never seen her wear the same one twice.

It was nearly four 'clock.

Tubby ordered another drink from the bartender, a Vietnamese man of about sixty—thin, tiny, wiry, who had been hired by the Bloat Country Club when he turned up in town as a refugee and it was learned that he had been a bartender in Saigon.

Tiny people make the best help, thought Tubby, in places like bars or restaurants. A waiter ought to be tiny, to get in and out among the tables without a lot of clumsy jostling and bumping into people.

The bartender spoke almost no English.

He fixed Tubby another bourbon and water. Tubby took it and turned back to the window to watch Carlena as she played in the water. Tubby's eyes glistened with tears as he watched her. She was so lovely, so sweet, so vibrant.

Tubby was deep in fantasy and did not hear his wife talking to him.

Mona Turmath, the rich man's daughter Tubby had married when she was just a little older than Carlena was now, had been pretty then, too, but she had changed, as had Tubby.

Where she had once been slim, she was now forced to wear a very tight girdle to pull in her pumpkin-like belly, and she used a rinse on her hair, sometimes Raven's Wing, sometimes Charcoal Embers, which made it too dark to look real.

Her face was puffy and lined with deep furrows and her teeth were orange, the color of a beaver's, from constant smoking of cigarettes. When she went to Hot Springs National Park in Arkansas, for the baths, the nicotine would sweat right out through her pores and stain the towels.

"... and you'll have to give me your keys," she was saying to Tubby, when, at last, he tuned her in.

"Mona Dell! Whatch you doing here? I just got in off the goff course!"

She paid no attention to what he was saying.

"... and that tank better not be empty, like it was last time!"

"Whatch that, honey?" asked Tubby.

"You haven't been hearing a thing I've said, have you?"

"Honey, I've been playing goff all afternoon."

"You've been sitting right in here at this bar, since I got here at two o'clock!" she said. "I could see you from the Colonial Room!"

Mona Turmath had been in the Colonial Room with some friends — Rock Tyler, Georgia Stackhouse, Cohen Rose and a queer dentist from Dallas, Texas — eating chicken *a la king* on toast points and drinking champagne until they were all about three sheets to the wind.

She had lost her car keys and broken her glasses and was having trouble standing up.

"Give me your keys," she said to Tubby. "You can get home with somebody else."

"I don't believe you're in any shape to try driving home, Mona

Dell," said Tubby.

"Give me those keys, Tubby Turmath!"

"I'll drive you home, Mona Dell," said Rock Tyler, who had joined them. "Come on, I'll take you home."

Rock Tyler was having an affair with Mona Turmath. Tubby Turmath knew about it but did not give one big damn.

Mona Turmath started toward the door with Rock Tyler. "You come right on home, Tubby!" she said as she left. "I mean it! Right on home!"

Tubby ordered another bourbon and water.

The bartender nodded in the direction of Mona Turmath and said, "Hot stuff, G.I.!"

"I hate her guts!" said Tubby. "You look yonder out that window at that girl on the diving board. Now, *that's* hot stuff, G.I.!"

The bartender smiled. He was tired. At five o'clock, he would get off work and then he could go out back behind the tennis courts to the 1957 Slip Stream house trailer that the Bloat Country Club provided for his living quarters and take a nap under the oscillating Emerson electric fan with the six-inch blades.

"I hate her guts!" repeated Tubby. "I hate her guts!" He turned up his drink and finished it. "It won't be long until I can get shed of her!"

He grabbed the bartender's coat at the lapels and pulled him close.

"I'll let you in on a secret, you little Gook! When that Roller Board Roadside Inn gets going out at the Cloverleaf, I'm going to be free! I'll have my own money, then. I got in on the ground floor because of her money, but I got the papers drawn up with Rafe Munger that cuts her out of the whole thing, altogether, soon as we open for bidness! It's just going to be me!"

"Hot stuff, G.I.!" said the bartender, when Tubby released him.

Tubby staggered toward the door.

"Don't you tell anybody what I said!" he yelled back at the bartender. "You keep your mouth shut! You heah?"

He walked across the parking lot, got in his car, started the engine, cut the wheels in the direction of the paved drive to the highway, misjudged the angle and took off across the lawn, knocking down a mimosa tree, planted in memory of the Korean War dead and not yet five feet tall.

27

Friday: The Bridal Shower

Friday afternoon, Patsy Rene Flatt, who had been in school with Davey Sue from the first grade all the way through high, and who had a birthday that was just three days different from Davy Sue's, gave her a Flexible China bridal shower.

Flexible China is the trade name for a line of kitchen bowls and tumblers made of plastic. They come with lids that fit tight and seal in the flavor. After a Flexible China bowl has been in use for a while, the edges get rough and you can cut your fingers just putting away leftovers.

Six weeks before, Patsy Rene's mother had given a Flexible China party and invited about twenty of Davy Sue's friends, but not Davy Sue, so that all the girls could do their shower shopping right then and there. Mrs. Flatt, as the hostess, would receive a percentage of the sales.

A Flexible China party is one where you are expected to buy Flexible China while you are there and pay down on it before you leave, balance due upon delivery.

A big woman had come from Rolling Fork in a mannish suit and sensible shoes to act as the Flexible China lady, which meant that she represented the Flexible China factory. She had demonstrated the use of various items, written up the sales, taken the money and would, in the end, also get paid a percentage for her part in the affair.

Fifteen of Mrs. Flatt's guests at the party had bought Flexible China items to give to Davy Sue, which meant that Mrs. Flatt got not only her percentage, but a special prize from the Flexible China lady — a twelve-piece set of Flexible China sherbet bowls.

Mr. and Mrs. Flatt pronounced their daughter's middle name "Reen."

"Patsy Reen! You come home right now!" her mother used to call down the street, when Patsy Rene and Davy Sue were little girls and it was time for Patsy Rene to go take her Tap and Twirl lesson.

Usually, Patsy Rene would be playing with other children in the lot behind the old ice house, and whenever the mothers of the other children heard Patsy Rene's mother calling her, they would also call their children home.

One mother had been coarse. She used to call to her son in foul language.

"Donnie Ray! Donnie Ray! Get your butt home!"

Donnie Ray had a tiny head, but not tiny enough to keep him out of the Navy. He had been in five years now, and every time he changed stations, he sent his mother a rayon kimono and his father a split bamboo fly rod, which the old man would use for whipping the dog, a Redbone hound named Tom, who would as soon bite as not.

Patsy Rene had decorated her parents' house with crepe-paper chains. The theme of the party was "Here Comes Love, Here Comes Marriage, Here Comes Davy Sue With A Baby Carriage," which caused everyone at the shower to suspect that Davy Sue was pregnant, which she was not.

Each guest had brought an item of Flexible China as a bridal shower gift. Davy Sue started unwrapping her packages.

First, a set of six plastic iced tea glasses, with a plastic rack for carrying and storage.

"I just love Flexible China ice tea glasses!" said one of the girls.

If a Flexible China tumber gets a rough edge — and it will if you wash it in a sink full of butcher knives — you can cut your lip right off your face, just going for a sip of tea.

"I like them a whole light better than those old hammered aluminum ones we have at home," said another girl. "Those things get so cold you can't hold them in your hand!"

"My brother was drinking out of an army cup once, in the Korean War, and it was winter, and you know how cold it gets in the winter, and he put that cold cup up to his lip and his lip froze right to it!" offered another girl. "They had to boil it right off his lip!"

"That won't happen with Flexible China!" said Patsy Rene.

Davy Sue continued to unwrap gifts.

The biggest one was a huge plastic globe for storing a roast turkey, and there was a bread box, a set of cannisters — containers for Flour, Sugar, Coffee and Tea — which all the girls called a "cannistry" set, and three lettuce crispers.

"If you don't have lettuce, you can use them for storing left-overs, like chili or navy bean soup," said the girl whose lettuce crisper had been opened last.

After all the gifts had been opened, the girls went into the kitchen where Patsy Rene had set out chicken salad sandwiches, cookies, and a punch made of ginger ale, lime sherbet and pine-apple juice.

For dessert, there were bowls of Heavenly Hash — a confection made of chopped marshallows, chocolate, pecans and cherries. There was also a plate of fudge, a chocolate cake and chocolate marble ice cream.

"Girl, you went all out!" said Davy Sue to Patsy Rene.

"You can do the same for me, only better, when I get married, with all Rafe, Jr.'s money!"

One of the girls eased up to Davy Sue and asked, "How far along are you?"

"What*ever* do you mean?" asked Davy Sue.

The girl pointed to the hand-lettered sign over the punch bowl.

"Here Comes Davy Sue With a Baby Carriage!" she said.

"Why, what are your talking about!" gasped Davy Sue. "You know I'm Saved!"

All the girls were interested in Bunny.

By now, everyone in town knew that Rafe, Jr. was being held in jail for totalling out a sporty little Pimp with factory air, for puking on a Stingray, and, incidentaliy, for rape.

"Are you going on your honeymoon with that cute proxy?" asked one girl.

All the girls giggled.

"He can be my proxy, any day!" said one of the girls, who was thought to be loose all through high, but who was never actually caught.

"Bunny Whitesides is just a proxy for the wedding," said Davy Sue. "After the wedding, he'll go his way and I'll go mine!"

"But Bunny's so cute!" said Patsy Rene. "I'd think of some

way to keep him around after the wedding, if it was me!"

The girls giggled.

"I had that on my mind, at first," said Davy Sue. "I really did."

"You mean you quit thinking about it?"

"I sure did!" said Davy Sue.

"But why?" asked Patsy Rene.

"I made my plans to marry Rafe, Jr., and I'm sticking to them!"

"How long will it be before Rafe, Jr. gets off... active duty?" asked one girl.

Davy Sue's eyes watered a little and everyone looked away.

"If Miss Effie Chad Reed could see you now!" said Patsy Rene, to get the party back on a festive note. "And you, her prize pupil!"

"That sweet old lady!" said Davy Sue. "I sure wish she could have been here!"

"I wanted to ask her," said Patsy Rene. "But you know she's still kind of off her head since Bunny picked her up that day at the Dog and Cat. They said they might have to give her shock treatments to get her to snap back."

"That poor old lady!" said Davy Sue. "Bunny feels so bad about skylarking with her!"

"How do you know how he feels?" asked the girl who was thought loose in high. "He can't talk. How do you know anything about him?"

"Bunny can hear like a bell!" said Davy Sue. "I know how he feels because Mr. Leaptrot can understand his sign language and Mr. Leaptrot tells me what he's saying. Mr. Leaptrot can talk to animals!"

"Where did those two come from?" asked the thought-to-be-loose girl. "How come they turned up right here in Bloat so close to your wedding? How come they don't seem to have any ties?"

"Mr. Leaptrot says his folks were circus people," said Davy Sue.

"Well, that explains it."

"Explains what?" asked Davy Sue.

"Explains why they both look so much like they just got off a county road force, somewhere!"

"Mildred Splinters! I'm ashamed of you, talking like that, and you a BTU!"

"Do you think Yvonne Hangman will get home in time for the wedding?" asked Patsy Rene.

"I think so," said Davy Sue. "That's what her mother told

me."

"That old lady'll tell you anything," said Mildred Splinters.

"And talk your arm off while she's doing it!" said Patsy Rene.

28

Friday: Yvonne Hangman Comes Back to Bloat

Yvonne Hangman, star of *Moonshiner's Daughter,* arrived in Memphis on a mid-afternoon flight from "the Coast," as they say in *Variety.*

With her was her manager, a cute little slicer wearing a suit made of brown canvas and a pair of green shoes, decorated with swatches of the plumage of a Mallard duck. He was carrying a brown leather purse on a strap over his shoulder and had a thin, clipped moustache.

His name was Chocco Popollino and he was some kind of Spic.

Yvonne Hangman had long, natural blonde hair and was tall and shapely, but she talked just like Davy Sue Merkle, Sula Measles or Patsy Rene Flatt.

"Chocco, run down yonder to the AVIS place and rent us a Cadillac convertible. And, puddin', be sure and try to get one that's purple outside and a dove grey inside!"

Chocco Popollino started for the AVIS counter, literally running, his leather heels clicking rapidly on the terrazzo floor of the Memphis airport.

He had been a hairdresser in New York, who also made pornographic movies for the Peep Shows, when he met Yvonne Hangman at a party given to raise money for Bangladesh. Under his direction, she had started making pornographic movies, among them a series about a young girl called the Whip Kitten.

First, they had made *Whip Kitten,* then *Whip Kitten in the Army, Whip Kitten in the Navy, Whip Kitten in the Air Force, Whip Kitten in the Foreign Legion, Whip Kitten Goes to College, Whip Kitten Goes West,* and finally, one directed by Yvonne Hangman herself, called *Whip Kitten Waits Table.*

There was good money in the Whip Kitten Series — for Yvonne, for Chocco, and for the swarthy men in the dark suits who controlled the distribution.

Yvonne Hangman and Chocco Popollino were headed south to Bloat, in a rented car. Chocco was driving. He wore a boy's size twelve and had trouble reaching the pedals.

"Why didn't you rent a Cadillac convertible, like I said?" asked Yvonne. "I ain't a bit happy, going back home in some little Jap-ass car!"

"It's a Moppet," said Chocco.

"What are the people in Bloat going to think when they see me pull up in this car? I told you to rent a Cadillac convertible with a purple outside and a dove grey inside!"

"It's all they had."

"This damn loadwagon don't even have factory air!"

"It's all they had, I'm telling you! All their big cars were already rented out! All of them! There's some spade church convention in town and they took all the big cars. This Moppet is all I could get!"

"Anybody that sees me in this car is gonna think I ain't made it big!"

"No, they won't."

"You don't know Bloat!"

"How long since you've been home?"

"Five years. Just at."

"Do any of these farmers down here know about you making skin flicks?"

"There ain't nobody down here knows about it! Where they gonna see one? You think they run them wide open at the Dot?"

"Maybe someplace else."

"Hell! Half of Bloat ain't never even seen a Volkswagen, much less a skin flick!"

"Somebody might know you're making skin flicks now, instead of that *Moonshiner's* junk."

"So what? It's all the moom pitchurs, ain't it?"
Outside of town, they passed the sign:

WELCOME TO BLOAT, MISSISSIPPI.
HOME OF YVONNE HANGMAN.

Yvonne made Chocco stop and take a picture of it.

They entered Bloat at the north end and drove slowly down Main Street.

"Did you ever see such an awful, dead town?" asked Yvonne. "I'm sure glad I don't have to stay here but one night."

"I don't know why you came down here at all!" said Chocco.

"I came back special for Davy Sue's wedding! She was my best friend all through school, even when I got kicked out in the seventh grade for getting pregnant. Back then, Davy Sue was the only one stuck by me. Poor Davy Sue! Marrying that no-count Rafe, Jr! He's one of the sorriest sons of bitches I ever run across in my life."

For the past two years, Yvonne Hangman had been trying to get rid of her Bloat, Mississippi accent and bring her voice down from the high keys.

She was taking expensive speech lessons and breathing exercises and was now able to say "It's been so nice meeting you" and "How wonderful to see you again" without sounding like a redneck.

"That's my momma's house, up yonder, Chocco,"said Yvonne. "The one with the sunflowers in the yard, where all them people are standing."

"Who are they? Fans?"

"I reckon!"

Yvonne jumped out of the Moppet and started hugging the townspeople who were waiting to greet her and tell her they remembered her when.

Five years away from Bloat, using expensive skin soaps and balms and lotions, sunning on the Pacific coast, learning to wear nice clothes, and having her hair done by Chocco Popollino (who did it even when he did not have to) had made Yvonne Hangman the loveliest young woman ever to grow up in Bloat, going as far back as when they took it away from the Indians.

"How wonderful to see you again!" she said, over and over.

Mrs. Faoud Honeycutt and Mrs. Fozell Sheath, two old women in men's houseshoes, watched Yvonne Hangman as she presided at

Yvonne Hangman and her mentor, Mr. Popollino.

her mother's house, hugging everyone and saying, "How wonderful to see you again!"

"Flo Ella sure talks pretty, don't she!" said Mrs. Sheath.

"Why, she talks just like Lady Astor!" said Mrs. Honeycutt, proudly.

Ricey Fitts was there, quacking obscenely on his duck caller.

"Star or not," he said to Coy Mink, Sr. "I figure she must be busted flat of her ass, coming home in a midget car driven by some half-pint Dago!"

When it came time for Coy Mink, Sr. to leave, he took Yvonne by the hand and sort of dragged her out on the front porch.

"How wonderful to see you again!" said Yvonne.

"They're running a Whip Kitten movie next week, up at the Blue Moon, in Memphis!" said Coy Mink, Sr.

"So, you know about *that*, do you!" she screeched, in a voice that set her own teeth on edge.

"I sure do!" said Coy Mink, Sr. "I never thought I'd live to see the day!"

"Well, you'd better not tell my momma about it, unless you want the Mafia all over your ass!"

She turned on her heel and went back inside the house. Only Davy Sue, Bunny and Mrs. Dermon, Yvonne's mother, remained.

Chocco Popollino had gone off to the Mink Motel, to rent a room for the night.

"Flo Ella, honey, your eyes is big as saucers!" said Mrs. Dermon. "Are you sure you ain't got a fever?"

"I'm all right, Momma! It's you I want to hear about! How's your legs?"

"I may get better but I ain't never gonna get well!" said Mrs. Dermon.

She went to the kitchen and brought back a tray of sandwiches — boiled frankfurters brushed with pickle relish, with one slice of bread folded around them.

"Honey, you have just fell off something awful!" she said to Yvonne. "Davy Sue, don't it look to you like Flo Ella has fell off?"

Mrs. Dermon went in to a back room to rest her legs, leaving Yvonne, Davy Sue and Bunny sitting on the sofa in the living room.

"You sweet pore thing!" said Yvonne to Davy Sue. "Having to marry that no-count Rafe, Jr!"

"I'm not having to marry him, Yvonne, honey," said Davy Sue. "I'm doing it 'cause I want to! Honey, Big Rafe is putting together a real estate deal that will make him the richest man in the county, and I'm going to be his daughter-in-law! I can put up with Rafe, Jr.

I didn't have no good looks like you did. All I could do was add up a column of figures, quick as a flash. I'm having to make the best for myself with what I have."

"It's a shame you can't marry this sweet boy, Bunny," said Yvonne. "What do you do, Bunny?"

"Bunny can't talk," explained Davy Sue. "He's a mute. He can hear like a bell, but he can't talk."

"Why you pore thing," said Yvonne. "You're about the best-looking man I've ever seen! It's all I can do to keep from hugging your neck!"

Bunny withdrew to a far end of the sofa, his fist doubled up behind his back.

"I'm just so glad you were able to come to the wedding, Yvonne," said Davy Sue. "I was afraid you couldn't get away, with all your commitments."

"You couldn't have kept me away," said Yvonne. "I wish I could do something to help you get out of here, to some place where you could live like a human being."

"Don't worry about me, Yvonne. I'm going to be rich! I'm going to be the daughter-in-law of the richest man in Titus County!"

"I hope so," said Yvonne. She looked at Bunny. "What about Bunny?" she asked. "What's going to become of him when this is all over?"

"I don't know," said Davy Sue. "I understand from his friend, Mr. Leaptrot, that they move around a lot."

"How'd you like to work for me, Bunny?" asked Yvonne.

Bunny smiled and nodded in agreement.

"Doing what, Yvonne?" asked Davy Sue.

"Acting in the movies!" said Yvonne. "Bunny can play the male lead in my next movie!"

"You hear that, Bunny? You're going to star in the movies!" said Davy Sue. "Oh, I'm so happy I could cry!"

Davy Sue and Bunny left, to attend an Eve of the Wedding Supper given by the Ramona Gullet Circle of the Nona Farnsworth League of the Order of the Eastern Star.

After they were gone, Yvonne picked up the telephone and called Chocco Popollino at the Mink Motel.

"Chocco, I've just met the best-looking man I've ever seen in my life! I want him for the male lead in my next movie, *Whip Kitten Goes to Mars.* You fix it! He's got some kind of partner, an old man named Leaptrot. You'll have to work it all out. When we leave here tomorrow, I want them to go with us."

Chocco said he would arrange it.

"He don't know anything about what kind of movies I make. I

didn't tell him a thing! His name is Bunny something and he's staying right there at the Mink Motel. Just look around. Find the only good-looking man there and it'll be Bunny!"

29

Friday: Rafe, Jr. and Marshal Catfield Discuss the Wedding

Rafe Munger, Jr. and Marshall Hazel Catfield were sitting in Rafe, Jr.'s jail cell, eating supper — chili beans and rice — and drinking beer.

One other prisoner, a man about fifty, who could not talk sense, and who slobbered and staggered when he walked, had been picked up on the streets of Bloat that afternoon and put in jail until he sobered up.

He was sitting on a bunk in the back of the cell.

Marshal Catfield and Rafe, Jr. were sitting at a table up near the front of the cell, so the marshal could hear the telephone if it rang. The marshal was showing Rafe, Jr. a stack of dirty pictures.

"Where'd you get these?" asked Rafe, Jr.

"Took them off an Atlanta lawyer that came through here about a year ago."

"How'd you know he had them?"

"I didn't know when I stopped him! It was just pure luck!"

"I don't get it!" said Rafe, Jr.

"I always stop any big cars, full of rich people, that come

through Bloat. You never know what you're going to find in a car full of rich people. They may have jewelry, luggage, cameras, tape recorders, you don't know what all, on them."

"How do you get away with stopping them?"

"Charge them with drunk driving. It always works. Rich people stay drunk, anyway. Don't you know that?"

"What about these pictures?"

"Fella came through here in a big Lincoln Continental. Weaving a little. I stopped him. Found them right there on the front seat."

"What happened to him?"

"Ten years at Parchman Farm. Interstate pornography."

"Is he still there?"

"He tried to escape one time. They had to shoot him in the knees. I hear the suh mitch is a cripple now."

"You got to keep the pictures?"

"You never know when they might need them for evidence!" Marshal Catfield laughed heartily.

"I didn't know you got to keep the pictures," said Rafe, Jr.

"What do you think happens? That they get destroyed or some damn-fool thing like that? When the law takes up dirty pictures, they just change hands."

Both men laughed.

The other prisoner got up off the bunk and staggered toward the marshal.

"I w-w-want to g-g-get out of here," he said, in a slurred, halting speech.

"Get back on that bunk 'til you sober up, suh mitch!" said the marshal. "Go on now! Don't gimme no more trouble about getting out of here 'til you sober up!"

"Who is he?" asked Rafe, Jr.

"Damned if I know. I found him at noon today, staggering along Main Street. Nobody in town knew who he was."

"Drunk?" asked Rafe, Jr.

"Looked to me more like he'd smoken dope!"

The two men watched the television a while.

"This time tomorrow," said Marshal Catfield, "you'll be a married man."

Rafe, Jr. slammed his fist down into his plate of chili beans and rice.

"You know I don't want to talk about the wedding!" he said.

"Sorry. I just thought people were supposed to be happy about their wedding."

"That wedding was not my idea! You've seen Davy Sue Merkle. Who do you know in their right mind would want to marry her?"

The marshal pondered that one a moment. "No one. No one that I know of," he said.

"You're damn right!" said Rafe, Jr.

"They say she's good at figures."

"Marrying Davy Sue is my daddy's idea. Wadn't none of mine!"

"Why would he want to marry you off to Davy Sue?"

"He wants her in the bidness. He wants somebody he can trust to keep the books. He all but came out and told me that!"

"You don't love her?" asked the marshal.

"Hell, no, I don't love her!"

"They say there's nothing better than a piece of ass off a woman you love."

"I never loved nobody!" said Rafe, Jr.

"You don't have to marry her, do you? She ain't... is she?"

"Are you kidding? Hell, no, I don't have to marry her!"

"Then why are you doing it?"

Rafe, Jr. threw a beer can against the wall. "My damn daddy, that's why! There's no standing up to him!"

"Boy, getting married is going to put an end to the kind of life you been leading," said the marshal. "Marriage puts an end to everything!"

"I know it!" said Rafe, Jr.

"If I was you, I'd just tell them, 'Hell, no, I won't get married!' I mean it! Put your foot down!"

"He'd throw me out. He'd cut me off! I'm no fool!"

"You damn well *are* a fool, boy!" said the marshal. "A DAMN fool!"

"I wish I was free," said Rafe, Jr. "I wish I could start over! I wish I was free!"

"What would you do?" asked the marshal. "What is it you'd do if you was free? What is it you'd be?"

Rafe, Jr. twisted his face into a maniac's smile.

"I wouldn't be a developer, like my daddy! Not a developer! Not a bidnessman!"

"What *would* you like to be? asked the marshal.

Rafe, Jr.'s face broke into a peaceful light.

"There's one thing I've always wanted to be. One thing I'd like to do!"

"What is it, boy?" asked the marshal, excitedly. "What is it?"

"Just one thing! I'd like to be ... an Arthur Murray dance teacher!"

The other prisoner got up off the bunk again and started

staggering toward the marshal.

"I w-w-want out of here!" he said, slurring the words.

"You drunk suh mitch!" said the marshal. "I told you, already, you're gonna stay in here 'til you sober up!"

"D-d-d-runk? I'm not d-d-d-runk! I'm s-s-simple!"

30

Friday: Davy Sue Says Goodnight to Rixie Leaptrot and Bunny

Davy Sue and Bunny left the Eastern Star supper at nine-thirty and walked slowly up Main Street, from the Masonic Hall toward the Mink Motel.

Bunny picked up every heavy object along the way and held it over his head long enough for Davy Sue to count ten. At the corner of Main Street and Rector Avenue, he picked up a two-wheel trailer filled with one cubic yard of gravel. Two men in the pool hall across the street saw him do it.

"Who is that Tom fool?" asked one.

"That's the proxy! They say he's strong as an ox!"

"They ought to get that boy on the Grand Ole Opry!"

Rixie Leaptrot was sitting on the sidewalk in front of the Mink Motel, taking in the night air in one of Mink's slat wood chairs.

"This is your last night as a free woman, Davy Sue," said Rixie Leaptrot. "You ought to be out kicking up your heels!"

"I ain't got time to kick up heels, Rixie! I got to hurry home and get my hair done!"

"This time of night?"

"The lady that runs Darla-Rells House of Hair is staying open late tonight to set my hair as a wedding present," said Davy Sue. "I'll have to sit up all night in a chair so it won't get out of place."

Davy Sue took Rixie Leaptrot's hands in hers.

"I'm sure going to miss you and Bunny!" she said. "You two are just about the best friends I got in the world!"

"We're going to miss you, too, Davy Sue. Won't we, Bunny?"

Bunny nodded in agreement.

"What about that little problem we talked about in the park?" asked Rixie Leaptrot.

"You mean, the feelings I was having for ... someone else?"

"That's it. I promised you I'd think of something, but so far..."

"Don't worry about that, Rixie. That's not a problem, anymore."

"It's not?"

"I'm going for the money!"

"Bless your heart, Davy Sue!" said Rixie Leaptrot.

"It's money that counts, Rixie. I know a girl from Port Spuds who was as poor as I am until she married a baby doctor. Now, she can buy all the magazines and Lifesavers she wants."

31

Saturday: Wedding Day in Bloat

Mid-morning.

Rixie Leaptrot was in his room at the Mink Motel, packing the new clothes Big Rafe had bought him and the other things he had collected during the past week in Bloat, getting ready to move on after the wedding. He had a dozen sterling silver dinner forks from Rosecliff, the old plantation home of the Alexander brothers, and six big bath towels from the Mink Motel. Rixie Leaptrot folded up towels around silver and stuffed them into the new Oxnalite suitcase he had bought at Mumm's Dollar Discount.

Bunny was in the bathroom, shaving.

"We'd better make tracks as soon after the wedding as we can, Bunny. After it's all over and done, they won't need us around here. We'll just be in the way. They might even try to go back on us with that Dog and Cat stick-up. That Big Rafe, he said he'd arrange it for us to get a job with a friend of his, a fella name of Juan Wolfe, who runs a roofing paper factory in Jackson. He said we could get six cents a hundred, stacking shingles.

"I guess that's it, then. Jackson, Mississippi, it'll be. I'd rather drift on up to Memphis. They got three blood banks there, three missions, too. They got one, Brother Big Time's, where they give you all the bread you can eat. Day-old. I'd rather go to Memphis, at that, but I guess we'd better go to Jackson and try that job.

"This last week, we've been living like kings. Three meals a day at the Spit. New clothes. It's going to be hard, drifting again. In and out of jails. I figure I might oughta try that shingle stacking job. You and me. Stacking shingles. Might not be so bad."

Bunny had come out of the bathroom and was putting on his lime-green tuxedo while Rixie Leaptrot was talking.

"Yeah, Bunny. I'm getting too old to spin the night in missions. All that coughing. Puking. Fights. I need to get off the road. Get a place of my own. The only way to do that is get a job. Much as I hate to. Yes, sir! It's you and me! Stacking shingles!"

Bunny touched Rixie Leaptrot's shoulder to get his attention. When he had it, he started an animated series of movements with his arms and hands.

"What's that?" asked Rixie Leaptrot. "A job in the movies? Yvonne Hangman wants you to work for her? Well, I'll be damn! In the movies? Doing what?"

Bunny answered that he did not know.

"Work around the lot, I reckon," said Rixie Leaptrot. "Heavy lifting, that kind of thing."

Bunny shook his head and made some more movements with his hands.

"Being *in* the movies?" exclaimed Rixie Leaptrot. "IN THE MOVIES?"

Bunny nodded.

"In the movies! Bunny, that could mean real money! In the movies! I wonder, doing what?"

Bunny did not know.

"In the movies," repeated Rixie Leaptrot, as he set out his "road" clothes, now cleaned and pressed, to change into after the wedding.

The two men finished dressing in their lime-green tuxedos, then placed boutonnieres made of white chicken feathers in their lapels.

Nearly noon.

Things were slow at the Spit Cafe.

Only Mom, the waitress, Coco Seifert, the rich planter's daughter, and Buster, the routeman for Fay's Nuts and Chips, were there.

Buster was sitting at the counter.

Coco Seifert was in the back, by herself, drinking beer and looking off in the distance.

"She's not going to the wedding," said Mom to Buster. "Look at her back there, ruby jewels all over her fingers and drinking that beer like it was water! She thinks she's better than we are!"

"Are you going to the wedding?" asked Buster.

"I can't get away. I've got to keep the Spit open. Me and the cook. I wanted to go. They won't be nobody in here until after it's over, but the boss said no. I got to stay open for transients."

"Miss Coco's not going. She could watch the Spit," said Buster.

Mom liked the idea. "Miss Coco, Buster here says you could watch the Spit while I went to the wedding."

Coco Seifert was disturbed from her reverie.

"What did you say?" she asked.

"Buster here says I could go to the wedding if you'd watch the Spit."

"Miss Seifert does not wait table!" said Miss Seifert.

"See!" said Mom to Buster. "Right there! She thinks she's better than me! She thinks there's something low-class about waiting table! Rich bitch!"

"I still plan to wind up getting me some of that," said Buster, of Miss Seifert.

"What would you want with a woman that old, you still in your thirties and her nearly sixty?" asked Mom.

"Everybody to his own taste, said the old woman when she kissed the cow," said Buster.

"That's cute!" said Mom. "I never heard that one before. That's real cute!" Mom turned grim. "Seriously, you want to know what Miss Coco gave Davy Sue for a wedding present? You really want to know? You'll never believe it!"

"What was it?" asked Buster. "Something dirty?"

"No, it wasn't dirty! It was ugly! Ugly in place of dirty!"

"Well, what was it?"

"A pitchur!"

"A pitchur?"

"A drawd pitchur. She bought it up at Memphis at that Art Academy. Just a little old pitchur, drawd with a fat pencil! A woman sitting in a chair with a monkey on her lap. Framed and everything."

"Don't sound like much."

"It wadn't much! It wadn't nothing! Ain't that awful! With her money, Coco Seifert could have given Davy Sue something nice. She could have bought her two or three of those baby-blue fiberglass blankets they got down at Mumm's Dollar Discount. Have you ever seen them?"

"Naw."

"You talk about something that would keep you warm!"

Mom left the counter to go into the kitchen and make sure Altie, the cook, was frying breaded shrimp and not just sitting on her ass, like most of the time.

Buster went outside to his truck and brought in a big cardboard box filled with fifteen-cent packages of dry roasted peanuts, salted pecans, fried cashews, potato chips and Taco Fritters and started to the back of the Spit, where Miss Seifert was sitting in her gold lamé jumpsuit and her gold lamé slippers with the curled-up toes.

She was wearing lots of rubies and diamonds and gold bracelets and was bathed in Mitsuko perfume.

"You ain't going to the wedding, Miss Coco?" asked Buster.

"I hate weddings. I've had five — four — what is it? — four or five of them myself."

"I didn't know you'd been married that many times!" said Buster.

"The first time I got married, my picture was in the *New York Times*!"

"Well, I'll be damn!" said Buster.

"I sent Davy Sue a gift. A beautiful drawing of a mother and her child. But I will not go to the wedding!"

Buster moved closer to Miss Seifert.

"Let's you and me slip down to the Mink Motel and spin the afternoon!"

"I've told you before, young man, you're too old for me!"

"There ain't no such thing as too old!"

Miss Seifert smiled and took a sip of beer. "Oh, yes, there is!" she said.

"This Spit is going to be dead, until after the wedding! Come on! Let's slip down to the Mink! Come on, Miss Coco!"

"'Come away, O human child!/To the waters and the wild...'"

"What's that?" asked Buster.

"A poem."

"Come on, Miss Coco! We won't have another chance like this, for a long time!"

"Are you perfectly serious?"

"Yes, ma'am!"

"Then, why not? There's a dance in the old girl yet!"

Coy Mink, Jr. looked rumpled.

His usually neat hair was mussed and his black necktie was knotted very tight, like someone had been pulling for dear life on the end of it.

Someone had. The late Coy Mink, Sr.

Coy Mink, Jr. had done it!

He had slipped up on his parents as they watched a dozen six-year-old girls in red velvet costumes tap dance on Memphis television, and had let them have it with the twelve-inch hunting knife given him by the Methodist Church when he made Eagle Scout.

Coy Mink, Jr. had expected to feel happy, but he did not. He felt strange. Not scared. Not tired. Not weak. Not sick or played out — just overwhelmed by the task still before him.

He meant to kill every person on earth but he knew he would be caught and locked up long before he could even make a dent in Titus County, let alone Mississippi or the Mid-South.

Coy Mink, Jr. knew at the start that his project was hopeless, but he was going to try, anyway.

He would go as far as he could and do as much good work as the Lord would allow him.

When Coco Seifert and Buster entered the Mink Motel, Coy Mink, Jr. was sitting behind the desk, honing the hunting knife against the sole of his shoe.

"We'd like a room, please," said Coco Seifert.

She was the only woman in Bloat who would walk into the Mink Motel with a man, in broad daylight, and ask for a room. That was because she was rich and had been brought up differently and had graduated first in her class at Sophie Newcomb in New Orleans.

"I know him!" said Coy Mink, Jr. "He's the Nut and Chip Man!"

There was a selection of Fay's chocolate-covered graham crackers on a table by the Coke machine. The chocolate was made of paraffin and would stay on forever, without going bad. It was said to have a good shelf life.

"Buster's tired and wants a room for the night," said Coco Seifert.

"He's not going to the wedding?" asked Coy Mink, Jr.

"I want to," said Buster, "but I think I'm too tired."

Coco Seifert signed the register and gave Coy Mink, Jr. four dollars for the room.

"Number seven," said Coy Mink, Jr., taking a key off the wall and handing it to her.

"That boy looks crazy to me!" said Buster to Coco Seifert, as they climbed the stairs. "Did you see the way he was drawing that big knife back and forth across the sole of his shoe?"

"Don't worry about him," said Coco Seifert. "He's taking treatments."

Coy Mink, Jr. watched Coco Seifert and Buster climb the stairs to the room.

"Tired, my foot!" he thought to himself. "They're going in

there to do sex!"

Coy Mink, Jr. may have been an Eagle Scout but he knew enough about doing sex to know that people pass out and slumber after it is over.

He took the master key down off the wall and put it in his pocket.

When Big Rafe picked up Rixie Leaptrot and Bunny in his big Mercury with the fancy options, to take them to the wedding, a well-dressed woman about Big Rafe's age, wearing the type of clothes a refined woman would wear to an afternoon wedding at the bride's home in the South, was sitting in the seat next to him.

"How do, Mrs. Munger," said Rixie Leaptrot.

Big Rafe beamed inwardly.

It was not his wife, but a middle-aged character actress, a member of the resident company of the Circuit Playhouse in Memphis, a woman who specialized in playing refined Delta women, whom Big Rafe had hired for a flat fee of one hundred dollars to attend the wedding with him and pretend to be his wife.

The real Mrs. Munger was at home. She refused to attend the wedding.

"I'd rather see my boy branch manager of a Western Auto than married to that snake chunker's daughter!" she said as Big Rafe had left the house.

It would work, hiring the actress. Big Rafe knew it would.

The only one he had to fool was the Executive Vice-President of Roller Board Roadside Inns, who had never seen Mrs. Munger, and who would just assume the actress was Mrs. Munger, as had Rixie Leaptrot.

Everyone else at the wedding would assume she was an out-of-town relative.

Big Rafe drove three blocks down Main Street, turned left at the old ice house, and they were at the bride's home.

It was small, four rooms on a slab, with white asbestos siding, across the street from Waco's Superette and next door to a beauty parlor and a taxidermy and bookkeeping service. The front yard was unkept. It had not been raked since last fall and what Bermuda had once been there had long since been choked out by clumps of Snoozy Grass, with tall shoots and sticker balls on the ends, that would dig right into your skin if you brushed against them.

Big Rafe and his party went around back and entered the house through the kitchen door.

Although there was still a half-hour before the wedding, the house was packed with guests.

The living room had been decorated with banks of flowers, Gypsophila, Widow's Wart, Jack-of-the-Dell, Ash Roses, Purple Pompom and Puppy's Cup, arranged in white wicker baskets borrowed from Mutt Brothers Funeral Home.

Mrs. Merkle took charge of Bunny.

First, she made him wet his hair, then she combed it, parting it on the other side, then she pinned a sprig of Dutchman's Britches in his lapel and splashed Avon's Cuban Man Scent cologne all over his face. Then she stashed him in the front bedroom.

"Now you stay in here, out of sight, until I motions for you. That'll be right after Cousin Buddy starts to sing 'Because' and about the time Davy Sue comes down the stairs and starts through the hall, heading toward the preacher."

"Where's Daddy Merkle?" asked Big Rafe of Mrs. Merkle. "Out campaigning for the school board?"

"Poor Daddy!" said Mrs. Merkle. "He's out in the garage. His teeth didn't get here yet, even though we called Greyhound twict. He's been meeting ever bus from Memphis for over a week, on the chance his teeth's wrapped up in a package on it."

Rixie Leaptrot shook hands with Bunny.

"This is it, Bunny! Just stay here until the lady motions and walk out slow and stately up to that platform in the living room and stand there until the bride shows up. When the preacher asks if you do, just nod. Tomorrow, we'll be on our way to the big time, you in the movies and me along as your handler."

Bunny nodded, smiled and picked up a television set, a big floor model with a real walnut cabinet — it was that old — and in a spirit of celebration, lifted it over his head, as high as it would go before touching the ceiling. A ceramic elephant, green with red glass eyes, that had been sitting on the television set, slid off and broke when it hit the floor.

"Devilment!" screamed the bride's mother. "That's a SIGN! Devilment! I'd better run out back and tell Daddy Merkle!"

When she was out of the room, Rixie Leaptrot leaned over to Bunny and whispered, "They may try to make us pay for that elephant! Try and keep down that skylarking until we can get out of here, will you now, Bunny!"

Wolfena Poppenbarger, the Society Editor of the *Titus County Tomcat*, entered the front bedroom and saw Bunny.

"Oh, Bunny!" she exclaimed. "You look good enough to sop in hot butter and hug red raw!"

Bunny smiled and gave a little bow.

At that moment, the bride's father, Daddy Merkle, independent candidate for the school board, running on the platform "Every Man His Own Bible Prophet!", entered the front bedroom, a fat, squirming copperhead snake coiled around his arm.

"The devil has been in here," he screamed, wild-eyed. "I must cleanse the chamber, as did Moab in the cave of the Sybarites!"

He let the snake play around the television set until the devil was purged, then he left, going outside through the living room, where the guests were gathered.

Many of them screamed when they saw the snake.

In the front bedroom, Bunny pantomimed an act of violence on the snake and asked Rixie Leaptrot's permission to perform it.

"Not that snake, Bunny! That'd be saccerligious."

Bunny looked downcast.

"I'm leaving you now, Bunny," said Rixie Leaptrot. "When that woman motions, you walk out there real pretty and stand still until the bride gets to you."

Rixie Leaptrot walked into the living room and mingled with the guests.

Everybody was there: All the parties to Big Rafe's Roller Board Roadside Inns deal, Davy Sue's brother Frank and his wife Juney Garland, all of Davy Sue's high school friends, Miss Effie Chad Reed, in her wheelchair, the hired Mrs. Munger, and the Executive Vice-President of Roller Board Roadside Inns, wearing the only necktie in the room not knotted at the factory.

A woman in pink eyeglasses opened the bathroom door and was instantly attacked by the Merkle family dog, who was bad and had been shut away there. Davy Sue's little brother, Motto, grabbed him, dragged him outside and forced him into the family car — a Plymouth with all the stuffing out of the seats.

The dog weighed over a hundred pounds and was one part Chow, with a blue tongue.

Rixie Leaptrot wandered into the kitchen, followed by Wolfena Poppenbarger.

Two card tables, side by side, were set up in the kitchen, and covered with a cloth to form the buffet. One table was higher than the other. The centerpiece was a real stuffed squirrel with a hickory nut in his mouth. There was a plate of finger sandwiches on one side of the squirrel and a bowl of punch on the other. The sandwich bread was dyed pink and blue with food coloring and the crusts had been removed.

Rixie Leaptrot reached for a sandwich and Wolfena Poppenbarger slapped his wrist.

"Not until AFTER the ceremony!" she said. "The bride and groom will come in here and receive. Do you know this is the first proxy wedding I've ever worked? It's surely going to be the wed-

Daddy Merkle was a snake-chunking preacher.

ding of the season! Have you ever seen so many beautiful florals? Delphiniums, and Sycconinniums, and such beautiful John O'Groat's Breath! And the tasting table! Isn't it lovely? Those sandwiches are just gorgeous! Tuna fish and pimento! But the bread is dry. Like sandpaper. They were made last night and left to stand! But the punch is just heavenly! I believe it's grapefruit juice and Coca-Cola. Well, it could stand just a little more ice! And the banana bread! Just perfect! Well, almost. I think they put just a pinch too much ground smug in the batter. Oh, I see Mrs. Heinrich had brought some of her famous pastry! Mrs. Heinrich, she's some kind of Norse woman — big, beefy, but so glad to help. Every time there's a wedding in Bloat, she bakes ox-blood muffins and sauerkraut cake for the tasting table. I do think Davy Sue made a mistake when she asked her cousin to sing. He's a perfectly sweet boy but he's so tongue-tied you can't understand a word he says..."

"Do tell," said Rixie Leaptrot.

"...I mean it! I said at the time, they ought to have his tongue clipped, but who's going to listen to an old-maid news hen when it comes to medicine? You're a great friend of the proxy, aren't you? Tell me, who is he, really? I hear from one of the Alexander brothers that his father is the richest man in Arkansas. Is it true that Toddy Alexander tried to borrow a hundred thousand dollars from him? Can I use that in my story?"

Brother Buell Mealer arrived outside the house, in his Ford Pinto. He was going to perform the wedding ceremony in the place of Brother Pond, who was reported to be "doing better" at the Mental Health Center in Oxford.

Brother Mealer got out of his car and walked up to the front door of the house.

"What Joy Today!" he boomed, to no one in particular, and let the Merkle family dog out of the Plymouth. It ran inside and bit Miss Effie Chad Reed, bringing blood and putting her back into shock.

Ten minutes before the wedding.

Those who could not get inside the house were peeking in the windows, trampling the Portulacca.

Brother Mealer, standing alone in the living room, swept his arm around and said, "What Joy Today!" and knocked over a white wicker basket of Sweetheart's Posy, Gloxinia, and Baby's Finger.

"More devilment!" muttered the bride's father and he pushed through the crowd, heading out to the garage and the snakepen.

He had been so busy he had not changed clothes for the wedding and still had on a polyester khaki-colored workshirt with TERMINIX on the back.

The Executive Vice-President of Roller Board Roadside Inns eased his way through the crowd and stood beside Big Rafe.

"It's a beautiful wedding," he said. "I know you're very proud to be getting such a smart daughter-in-law."

The Executive Vice-President extended his hand to the actress hired to impersonate Mrs. Munger and said, "How do you do, Mrs. Munger?"

Big Rafe smiled to himself. When it came to pulling the wool, he was it, all by himself. A man would have to get up in the middle of the night to get the best of Rafe Munger.

The Executive Vice-President took Big Rafe's hand and patted it softly.

"I was awfully sorry to read about your boy in the Memphis paper," he said. "So sorry. Who would have thought the Mafia had its tentacles out in a town like Bloat?"

"You read about my boy in the Memphis paper?" asked Big Rafe, turning white.

"It was quite a big story, written by some former reporter down here. I know it must have been an embarrassment to have it played up so prominently. I guess that's the price one pays for being well known in a town, like you are in Bloat."

"What did the paper say?"

"Everything, I presume. All about the attempt on the life of some state senator, the dope, the prostitution, the — you'll pardon me, Mrs. Munger — the rape. Tell me, do they expect that poor girl to live?"

"That was in the Memphis paper?" asked Big Rafe, in a whisper.

"They ought to do something about the newspapers being allowed to run stories like that."

"But what about the franchise?" asked Big Rafe, near unto death.

"I'm afraid that's out of the question. You know how our founder feels about good morals. It's no reflection on you, Munger, but we simply could not allow anyone associated with the crimes your son is accused of to be a franchise holder."

"No motel... here...?" asked Big Rafe.

"Oh, there'll be a motel here, all right. We awarded the franchise to the Stucco brothers."

"The Stucco brothers? But how did you have time? The financial statements? The bank references?"

"We didn't have to bother with financial statements for the

Davy Sue took little half-steps toward the preacher.

Stucco brothers. When Angelo Stucco came to see us, he brought a cashier's check for half a million dollars. Who would have ever thought there was that much money in tomatoes?"

"No motel...no motel...no motel," repeated Big Rafe, feebly.

He caught the eyes of Tubby Turmath and Dr. Dennis Dennis and slowly shook his head from side to side.

The bride's mother motioned to Bunny. He stepped out of the front bedroom, stood in the hall but an instant, turned into the living room and strode, slowly, majestically toward the preacher.

The bride's cousin Buddy, his DeMolay pin in his lapel, stepped forward, clasped his hands and started to sing.

"bee-TAWS, dod may do mine ..."

Big Rafe, at the back of the crowd, passed out and slid slowly to the floor, his face a dull blue. No one noticed him. It was probably his heart. He never got any exercise.

A bridesmaid, one of the six Rainbow Girls serving Davy Sue as attendants, stepped into the hall outside the bathroom door, reached up and pulled down the Fold-a-Way stairs to the attic. Davy Sue backed down them, bathed in sweat from having scrunched in the attic for over two hours. She turned toward the living room and began taking little half-steps toward the preacher, rolls of dust clinging to her dress, spiders in her hair and a spray of Monkey's Breath in her hand.

The End